THE GIRLS
OF CANBY HALL®

GRADUATION
DAY

EMILY CHASE

SCHOLASTIC INC.
New York Toronto London Auckland Sydney

No part of this publication may be reproduced in whole or in part, or stored in a retrieval system, or transmitted in any form or by any means, electronic, mechanical, photocopying, recording, or otherwise, without written permission of the publisher. For information regarding permission, write to Scholastic Inc., 730 Broadway, New York, NY 10003.

ISBN 0-590-40191-2

Copyright © 1986 by Patricia Aks. All rights reserved. Published by Scholastic Inc.

12 11 10 9 8 7 6 5 4 3 2   6 7 8 9/8 0 1/9

Printed in the U.S.A.   06

THE GIRLS
OF CANBY HALL®

GRADUATION
DAY

THE GIRLS
OF CANBY HALL®

CHAPTER ONE

"Here she is!" Dana shouted as Shelley burst into Room 407 of Baker dorm.

Dana and Faith had been impatiently awaiting their third roommate's arrival all afternoon and leaped up to greet her. Shelley dropped her suitcase on the floor so her arms were free to hug her two closest friends who had thrown their arms around her.

"I made it!" Shelley cried gleefully when they finally released her and she could breathe again.

"We knew you would," Faith said, picking up the suitcase and carrying it to Shelley's corner of the room.

"I wasn't so sure," Shelley said. "My whole family, which means my brothers Jeff and Larry, and my parents, and even the dog, Freckles, insisted on driving me to the airport in Des Moines. It was almost too much for our old station wagon, which we had trouble getting started, and then halfway there we got a flat. My brothers changed the tire in a jiffy, but Freckles got out of the car and with all the confusion decided he'd rather walk. It took the five of us at least twenty minutes to coax him back into the car. As it turned out the plane was on time and I made it with only five minutes to spare."

"Hope that wasn't the highlight of your midyear vacation," Dana remarked, grinning.

"Course not. The highlight was Paul — we're thicker than ever, but we've still agreed to date other people." She opened her suitcase and started unpacking.

Paul was Shelley's hometown boyfriend. They'd been going together in Pine Bluff steadily until she'd come to Canby Hall three years ago as a sophomore. Canby Hall was in Greenleaf, Massachusetts, about twenty miles from Boston, and it was very different for Shelley, who had lived in Iowa all her life. The first few weeks of school she thought she'd die of homesickness, but when she recovered and met Tom, a local Greenleaf boy, she admitted that maybe Paul wasn't the only boy in the world for her. Tom was fascinated by the theater, same as Shelley, and he was also a lot of fun. When they acted together for the first time in a play at Canby Hall, they became really close. Since then, her feelings for Paul and Tom had bounced back and forth like a Ping-Pong ball.

"It's nice that you can have Paul as your one and only and still go out with other boys. He's really understanding," Dana said. She stretched out on her bed, which was actually a mattress on the floor.

"You should talk, Dana," Shelley defended herself. "We'd need a scorecard to keep track of your boyfriends. For a while it was Bret Harper, all-American preppy. Then there was Randy, who works on his family's farm but looks more like a young Clint Eastwood than a farmer."

"We're still good friends," Dana said, smiling.

"I'm not finished yet! There was Mac McAllister, the handsome two-faced scoundrel, who happened to be a twin, and Terry O'Shaughnessy, our adorable dormmate — "

"Cease!" Dana squealed. "I admit it. I am kind of fickle. But to tell the truth I honestly wish I could settle on one guy like you have on Johnny, Faith. You two are perfect together. You even look alike!"

"That's right," Shelley piped up. "Both tall, dark, and handsome."

"By that you mean we're both black," Faith said with a chuckle.

"That's true, and you're a terrific-looking couple."

"Thanks, Shel." Faith patted her Afro haircut thoughtfully, and then added, "Doesn't mean Johnny and I haven't had our problems.

Problems that weren't anybody's fault."

Faith was referring to the fact that Johnny, who had graduated from Greenleaf High, was planning to become a police officer, and eventually a detective. Faith's father had been a police officer and was killed in the line of duty when Faith was ten years old. Her life had changed dramatically after that because her mother, who was a social worker, then became the sole support of the family — Faith; her older sister, Sara, who was in graduate school; and her younger brother, Richard, who was in tenth grade.

"But you know he's right for you. You're not torn in a zillion directions the way I am." Dana did her leg exercises while she spoke.

"Well, I did have a minicrush on Sheff Adams," Faith said a little sheepishly. Sheff was one of the three boys who had enrolled in Canby Hall the previous year and happened to be housed in what had formerly been servants' quarters in the basement of Baker. The girls referred to the experiment as "creeping coeducation," and it had been very successful.

"It's good to see that I'm not the only one who is torn asunder because of men," Shelley said dramatically, and her roommates laughed appreciatively.

"Not to change the subject, but how was your vacation, Shel?" Faith asked.

"Fantastic. Christmas parties and square dances and caroling or just plain pigouts every night. I think I must have gained at least four and a half pounds. I'm beginning to look like a Cabbage Patch doll."

Shelley was a pert, curly-haired blonde, and on the pudgy side. Since she was only five foot three and loved to eat, she had a constant battle with her weight. And as she pointed out, the weight was winning.

"Don't worry, Canby Hall's indescribable cuisine will take it all off," Faith assured her.

"I know. It's easy to go on a voluntary starvation diet here," Shelley said.

"That's why I came back from D.C. fortified with a fresh supply of soft pretzels and mustard. Who says you can't survive on junk food?" Faith took an enormous tin of pretzels and a jar of mustard off her dresser and passed it around.

"What did you do over vacation, Faith?" Dana asked, as she helped herself to a pretzel.

"Mainly I missed Johnny. And I spent a lot of time putting together my latest photographs. You know, I'd already applied to the University of Rochester, which supposedly has one of the best photography departments in the country — but they want to see my final portfolio. I have to do some more landscapes."

"With you being the photography editor of the *Clarion*, and undoubtedly the best photographer Canby Hall has ever had, the admissions people are probably fighting over who will write you their letter of acceptance."

Shelley took one of the pretzels, passed up the mustard, and whispered, "Dieting, you know."

Faith laughed and placed the goodies on the table in the center of the floor so everyone could help themselves. Then she walked to the window that overlooked the beautiful campus, which was beginning to have a soft, spring look.

"You know you'll get into Rochester," Dana said. "You've got the perfect credentials."

"Except for French."

"You don't need French to take pictures."

"No, but you're forgetting one major problem, and that's money. If I don't get a scholarship, I simply can't go."

Neither Shelley nor Dana knew what to say about that, and Faith quickly changed the subject. She didn't want to burden her roommates with her problems — certainly not the first day back!

"What did you do over vacation, Dana?" she asked. "Any new men?"

"As a matter of fact, a friend of my mother's introduced me to Norm Wiley, a freshman at New York University, and he kept me pretty busy."

"You might go into a little more detail," Shelley said. "What's he look like?"

"He's shorter than I am, even if I wear flats."

"And. . . ." Shelley was eager for more details.

"His skin is what you might call adolescent."

"You mean he has zits?" Faith sounded alarmed.

" 'Fraid so."

"Now don't tell me he's overweight." Shelley had finished unpacking, collapsed on her mattress, and was giving her complete attention to Dana.

"A little on the chunky side."

"Short, fat, and pimply," Shelley commented and the three girls cracked up.

"There must be something you're not telling us," Faith said. "Spill it."

"He's not what you'd call a Greek god, but he's got to be the most fun of anybody I've ever gone out with."

"That covers a lot of people," Shelley said.

"Not only that, but he has such an optimistic view of life. Likes to write, so we had that in common. Although my specialty right now is poetry, and he's more into humorous essays. He's really ugly/adorable. Not like any guy I ever liked before. I can see now what Casey sees in Keith."

Casey Flint lived down the hall. She was a tow-headed, dynamite barrel of fun who was always getting into trouble — often serious — and was a special friend of the girls of 407. Her first and only romance had blossomed the previous year with Keith Milton, one of the three new boys. Although Keith was partial to chartreuse shirts, and his glasses were grimy, and he was preoccupied with scientific concepts — all of which made him the complete nerd — he was sweet and lovable. He and Casey had flipped for each other.

"I can't see you with less than a borderline Adonis," Faith said.

Faith wasn't trying to flatter Dana, she was just being honest. Dana had emerald green eyes, thick, dark, shoulder-length hair, and a beautiful figure. Also, because her mother was a fashion buyer for a large department store in New York, Dana had an especially nice wardrobe. Her clothes were understated, but Dana could look terrific in a burlap bag. Whether she was running in a sweat suit, or studying for exams in her oldest jeans, she looked like the cover of a magazine. It was, indeed, difficult to imagine her with an "ugly," no matter how adorable.

"What else about him?" Faith asked.

"Well, he's great to talk to — about problems and stuff. I told him he should be a guidance counselor like our Michael Frank. Actually, he's a very good listener, but he's smart enough to know he can't solve what's bothering me."

"Dana, what are you talking about?" Shelley was always outspoken. More than once her roommates had accused her of having "hoof-in-mouth" disease.

"My father is putting pressure on me to live

with him and Eve next year and delay going to college. He's going to be living in Hawaii for another year, and he wants me to get to know my stepmother better. And also my new half-brother, Josh, who's over a year old. I've only met him once."

"You might have a wonderful time. Hawaii sounds so exotic, and you like Eve, don't you?" Shelley asked.

"She's okay — closer to my age than she is to my father's. I don't really know her that well."

"That's just what your father is saying. You can't blame him for wanting you all to get together. What about Maggie?" Faith asked.

Maggie was Dana's sister, two years younger than Dana, and she seemed much less affected by her parents' divorce. Unlike Dana, she adjusted very well to the break-up of the family. Dana, who was generally a very "up" person, always became glum when she had to cope with the fact that her parents were irreconcilably split.

"Maggie's going out there this summer, and I'm staying in New York with my mother. Problem is, I really love both my parents and I've got these conflicting loyalties. I just wish they'd stayed together."

"I guess everyone's got problems," Faith said. "If I don't get the scholarship, I'll be living at home, taking courses at the Photog-

raphy Institute at night, and waitressing
during the day. It'll be a good way to earn
money."

"I might join you in the waitressing career,"
Shelley said. "If I decide to move to New
York and try and make it in the theater, I'll
be waiting tables while I'm waiting to be
discovered."

"Let's not worry so much about the future,"
Dana said. "After all, we're seniors — women
of experience — and sometimes I can't believe
what we've been through together these past
three years. Remember how we had an armed
truce the first few weeks of school? We might
as well have taken a vow of silence, until
Alison straightened us out."

"Alison has got to be the best housemother
anyone ever had. She's so with it!" Shelley had
shed her traveling outfit, a bright red suit, and
was pulling on a pair of jeans.

"She's not much older than we are — and
looks more like a photographer's model than
an academic type," Faith said. "She's smoothed
out plenty of bumps over these past three
years. Made going to Canby Hall and living
in Baker a lot of fun."

"It's not over yet," Shelley remarked
casually.

"Not quite," Dana said.

"But almost." Faith was sometimes painfully realistic.

The three girls suddenly became silent, all

deep in their own thoughts — and all thinking the same thing.

"Well, we've got until June 6. That's G day." Dana tried to dispel the gloom.

"Yep, that's when we graduate, go out into the world brave and undaunted!" Shelley straightened her spine and pounded her chest.

"That's when we'll no longer be roommates," Faith said glumly. Then she quickly added, when she saw Shelley sink down on her mattress like a deflated balloon, "But we can promise to have a reunion every year for the rest of our lives."

"Neat idea," Dana agreed. "No matter where we are, we'll manage to meet every year on an appointed day."

"Even if it means missing one of my performances," Shelley said, giggling.

"Since the future is up for grabs, let's not talk about it for a while," Faith suggested.

"Right! Let's do something that's fun," Shelley said. "Since there'll probably be llama tailtips on the menu tonight, let's go to the Tutti Frutti and indulge ourselves in a double-dip ice-cream cone. As always, I'm dying of hunger."

"That's one thing, Shel, we can count on," Dana teased.

"Like the sun rising," Shelley said cheerfully.

"Like our forever friendship," said Faith.

CHAPTER
TWO

Patrice Allardyce, the headmistress of Canby Hall, was as usual impeccably dressed for the assembly meeting that took place the following morning before classes began. Her frosty blond hair swept back in a French twist, her perfectly manicured nails, and her well-tailored dark gray suit and crisp white blouse enhanced her image of a strict, unflappable administrator. P. A., as the students called her, was excruciatingly fair, but rules were rules, and not made to be broken.

Dana, Shelley, and Faith had set their alarm clock for seven o'clock, which gave them exactly twenty minutes to stumble out of bed, splash water on their faces, brush their teeth, and make their way to the auditorium where assembly was mandatory. They made it just in time, and settled in seats in the back row where they were less visible and hopefully could grab a few more minutes of sleep.

"P. A. will give her usual last-half-of-the-year speech. Wake me if I start snoring," Casey said as she slid into the aisle seat next to Faith, Dana, and Shelley.

"If we're still awake ourselves," Shelley promised, and slumped down, awaiting the traditional pep talk.

"Good morning, people," Ms. Allardyce began, and for the next fifteen minutes exhorted the students to reach for excellence in the last half of the year. "More than ever, it is incumbent that you extend yourselves, set your goals high, and live up to the standards that make Canby Hall renowned throughout the country."

"Blah, blah, blah . . ." Shelley mumbled under her breath. She sank farther down in her seat, as though that would enable her to blot out the rest of the speech, which she'd heard at least once every year for three years.

Ms. Allardyce ground to a halt at a quarter to eight — earlier than usual — and there was a collective sigh of relief from the girls of 407. They had been mercifully spared from hearing for the zillionth time a detailed description of what a Canby Hall education meant.

Casey had indeed fallen sound asleep, and Shelley gently nudged her. "It's over," she whispered. "We can go."

The girls prepared to make their escape, but Miss Allardyce was making an announcement: "Will the senior class please move to the front rows? All other students are dismissed."

"I knew it was too good to be true," Casey mumbled, and trudged down the aisle with her friends following.

When the senior class had arranged itself in the front of the auditorium, the headmistress looked them over.

"Nice to see you all looking so bright this early in the morning," she remarked with a forced smile. This was met with a sprinkling of polite laughter. It was Ms. Allardyce's feeble attempt at humor, which was a lot better than being on the receiving end of one of her scowls. A raised eyebrow on that patrician face could be as effective as a body blow. The headmistress was famous for the withering look, and perhaps that's why everyone was slightly intimidated by her.

"On a more serious note," she continued, "I want to talk about the responsibility of being a senior. You are models for our underclasspeople and must set an example. These last few months, more than ever before, you must be constantly aware of the effect you are having on our younger students. Do not assume that because you will be leaving these hallowed walls that you have a special license to break the rules.

"You have, of course, been allowed special privileges: Your curfew on Saturday night has been extended to midnight; you have been permitted to use extra rooms for senior lounges; and your sports are elective, rather than assigned, this semester. With privileges one must accept responsibility, something you would be wise to remember throughout life."

With that final admonition, she strode off the stage, and the seniors applauded half-heartedly. It was simply too early in the morning to be receptive to an inspirational talk.

"Did you get the feeling she was looking at me all through this?" Shelley asked, as the girls scrambled out of their seats.

"Don't be silly, Shel. It was me she was zeroing in on," Casey insisted. "I've had the distinct honor of being threatened with expulsion more than any other girl in the history of Canby Hall."

"There you go bragging again," Dana kidded her.

"You've survived so far, Casey," Faith said. "But don't tempt fate."

"Don't worry. I don't want to blow it after all I've been through. Besides, I don't think P. A. would kick any senior out now."

"She's a stickler for rules, though," Shelley said. "Who knows what she might do. . . ."

"It's not on my worry list, and right now I think I'll go to the senior lounge and have some coffee. Otherwise I'll nod off in class. Anybody care to join me?"

"We've only got twenty minutes 'til classes begin. Coffee sounds like a good idea," Shelley said.

"Me, too," Faith said.

"I think I'll do some running to get my motor going." Dana started to back away and bumped smack into Alison, who had been hurrying toward them.

"Before you do anything, you better say hello to me. I just got in this morning." Alison was looking radiant, her copper-colored hair glistening in the brilliant sun.

The girls let out whoops as though they hadn't seen their housemother for a year, rather than just a couple of weeks. They all took turns embracing her.

"Can't talk now, but I want to hear all about your vacations. Also, there's a meeting of the seniors in the lounge tonight at eight o'clock. We have to make plans for Arch Day."

"Arch Day? That doesn't take place until after finals," Dana said.

"I know, but there's plenty we have to do before then. Besides graduation, there's the school play, the final choral concert, the yearbook to close. . . . It's later than you think," Alison said, smiling, and ran off.

"That's just what we were thinking," Dana mumbled, and glanced at her roommates. The three of them shrugged their shoulders resignedly.

"Let's face it," Shelley said, "we are going to graduate."

"Not if we continue standing here," Casey joked. She was aware of the cloud that had descended on the group, and could sense why. "Let's move before they run out of coffee and before we get too sentimental."

"Casey, either you have ESP, or you were eavesdropping on our conversation yesterday," Dana observed.

"Neither. It's just that I have great powers of perception, so I know what you all are thinking and I feel the same way you do. Although there are plenty of reasons I'll be ecstatic about leaving Canby Hall, you three guys aren't one of them."

"You know something," Faith said, putting her arm through Casey's, "you're not nearly as tough as you look."

"You know something, Faith," Casey said, smiling, "your powers of perception aren't so bad, either."

The seniors gathered in a small room that served as a senior lounge. There were tables and chairs at one end of the room, and at the other was a grouping of comfortable stuffed chairs, sofas, and floor pillows. Alison had enlisted several students in setting up a refreshment table with cheeses, dips, and crackers, homemade cookies, and a variety of soft drinks. She knew that although the students had just had dinner, they could always eat.

If space had permitted, Alison would have invited the entire class to meet in her penthouse apartment on the top floor of Baker. It was decorated in rich earth colors, with splashes of bright yellow, hanging plants, modern posters, and shelves filled with books, pottery, and sculpture. Doby, her adorable cat, added to the homey atmosphere. The students considered Alison's apartment an oasis, and she welcomed them any time of the day or night.

Alison greeted everyone enthusiastically, and told them to grab a snack and settle down so that the meeting could get started. This was one occasion when no one had to be coerced, because Arch Day was something they all looked forward to and they wanted it to go without a hitch. They promptly sprawled on the chairs and floor, and Alison perched herself on a sturdy oak table so that she could see everyone and conduct the meeting.

"Glad you all made it," Alison said, "but I really wasn't worried. We all know how much Arch Day means to all the students, but particularly the seniors. To tell the truth, I feel honored that Ms. Allardyce asked me to be the coordinator for your class, and — "

Before she could go on she was interrupted by an ear-shattering round of applause. It was evident that everyone considered her the perfect choice.

"Thank you, thank you," she said, beaming, and held up her hands to quiet down the group. "As you know, Arch Day is in many ways as meaningful as graduation. The arch, bedecked with beautiful fresh flowers, will be constructed on the stage of the auditorium. All the other classes will pass through, symbolizing their being promoted to the next grade, and then return to their seats in the auditorium. The seniors, however, will pass through and exit off the stage and out of the school, symbolizing their departure from Canby Hall."

"Why do we have to have a meeting about all this? We know what it's about." Pamela Young, her elbows leaning against a hassock, and her long legs languidly stretched out in front of her, could always be counted on for her negative attitude.

Pamela was the daughter of a famous movie actress, Yvonne Young, and haughtily beautiful. Unfortunately, she thought she was better than anyone else. Perhaps it was envy, or maybe just a mean streak, that made her want to see everyone else in trouble — particularly the girls in 407. She couldn't bear their friendship with one another, and had even gone so far as to lie to break them up.

"I'm glad you asked that question, Pamela."

Alison knew who she was dealing with, and wouldn't allow herself to be rattled. "We do, indeed, know what Arch Day is about, but like any traditional celebration — Thanksgiving, Christmas, birthday parties — the ritual is similar every year, but each time it's unique. You have to admit that, don't you?"

"I suppose."

"Also, this class is really different. For starters, this is the first time we have boys. . . ."

"Let's hear it for the boys!" Casey shrieked.

Terry and Sheff stood up, dragged Keith to his feet, and together raised his arms over his head as though he'd just won a prizefight. Keith looked embarrassed, but couldn't stop smiling as all the girls cheered wildly.

When they quieted down, Alison continued: "We've got to decide what color robes you want, and who will write our class song, and who will decorate the arch. These are decisions we should make tonight so that we can get started. Mrs. Elliot Winship, who is a former alumna of Canby Hall, and presently on the board of trustees, has been so devoted to Arch Day that she will foot the bill for all the costs, providing they're within reason."

For the next hour they batted ideas about the robes back and forth, and after a closed ballot it was decided on a cool shade of green. "A wonderful choice," Alison said. "Happens to be one of my favorite colors.

"Glad it wasn't pink — never would have gone with my hair," Terry quipped, and everyone groaned.

Then Alison asked who would be interested in writing the class song. Only Dana and Terry volunteered, which pleased both of them. Terry whispered to Dana, "I'm glad there are only two of us because they say 'A camel is a horse made by a committee.' "

"One final thing before the meeting is over," Alison said. "We should decide on the decorating committee, which will be responsible for setting up the arch, trimming it with flowers, and making any other embellishments that would be appropriate."

Shelley's hand shot up, along with several others, and Alison looked pleased. "That does it for now," she said, "but there's just one more thing." She stared directly at Faith, and added, "I hope our star photographer will take pictures of the work in progress."

"I'd love to," Faith said. "It might be a good photo essay for the yearbook."

"Terrific idea, Faith. Now I think we've got a good start, and if you'll polish off the refreshments, I'll consider this a very successful meeting."

The seniors milled around, finished off the food, buzzed about the plans, and then drifted back to their rooms.

"Arch Day is my favorite ceremony at

Canby," Shelley said as she climbed the stairs with Dana and Faith trailing. "It's really just for the students and nobody else."

"Gives us something to look forward to," Dana agreed. "I'm glad we're all involved."

"It really means things are coming to an end," Faith murmured.

Shelley and Dana stopped dead on the staircase and glared at her. "It just slipped out," she apologized. "There's plenty of time left."

The girls nodded their heads in mutual support and continued climbing. In their heart of hearts, they knew Faith had reminded them of the unavoidable truth.

CHAPTER THREE

"I got the part, I got the part!" Shelley's voice could be heard before she was seen. Then she crashed into 407, tossed her books on her mattress, and twirled around the room.

"That's fantastic," Dana said. She had just showered and shampooed her hair after an afternoon run. Even though she was wrapped only in a towel, and her hair was dripping wet, Dana stretched out her arms to Shelley and the two of them pranced around the room.

"Congratulations, Shel," Faith mumbled.

She was halfway out the window, taking pictures of the campus. There were only five days left before she would have to send her landscape pictures to the University of Rochester. She'd taken dozens of rolls, but nothing satisfied her. Faith was aware that her talent was directed more toward portraits and human interest and feature photos than it was toward scenery. But she knew the competition to get into the university was tough, and to get a scholarship. . . . Every time she thought about it — which was at least once each hour — she was filled with dread.

Shelley had flipped on her radio to a rock station, and she and Dana were gyrating to the music. "Come join the fun," Shelley hollered, as she brushed by Faith.

"In a minute," Faith said. "I want to finish this roll."

"All work and no play. . . ." Dana was breathless, and playfully slapped Faith on the shoulder.

"I said in a minute," Faith snapped.

"Well, hurry up and close the window. I'm freezing to death," Dana pleaded.

Faith took a few more shots, closed the window, and then slowly backed into the room. "It might be wise if you put on some clothes, Dana. Then you wouldn't be so cold."

Dana didn't say a word, which was her way of handling her irritation with Faith.

The record had ended, and the disk jockey was babbling away, so Shelley turned off the radio. In mock exhaustion, she threw herself onto the bed.

"Don't fight girls. It's all my fault. But I was so excited about getting the role that I had to let off some steam."

Faith thoughtfully put her camera on her desk and slumped down on the chair. "I'm sorry, guys," Faith apologized. "I guess I'm so anxious about college that I can't think of anything else."

"Why don't you have a cut-off day — like today. You've been hanging out of windows all week, and maybe you're just being too much of a perfectionist." Dana towel-dried her hair and looked at Faith with concern. She realized that Faith was really worried, and that she hadn't been very sympathetic.

"That's probably good advice," Faith admitted, and the two girls smiled at each other. Their momentary tiff was quickly forgotten, and Shelley was soon regaling them with details of the play.

"It's called *You Can't Take It with You* by George S. Kaufman and Moss Hart. And the best thing is that Tom is going to be in it!"

"I'd love to hear more details, but I've got choral rehearsal now." Dana had miraculously finished blow-drying her hair and gotten dressed in two minutes in a new kilt and green turtleneck sweater her mother had just sent her.

"I thought we'd have a celebration — you know, me getting the part and everything. Maybe we can go to Pizza Pete's later," Shelley suggested.

"Later I'm meeting Terry for a brainstorming session about the Arch Day song. We haven't even decided what music we're going to put the words to." Dana zipped up her parka and pulled the hood over her head.

"How about you, Faith?" Shelley asked hopefully.

"Sorry, but I'm going to develop this roll and see what I come up with. I'm not sure how long I'll be in the darkroom, so I really can't make any plans for later." Faith got ready to leave, too.

"Okay," Shelley sighed, and started straightening her dresser drawers. Whenever Shelley was upset she did some cleaning up.

"See ya," Dana said, and headed for the door. She was so intent on not being late that she didn't seem to notice that Shelley's feelings had been hurt.

"Wait a sec," Faith called to Dana. "I'll walk you as far as the music building."

Shelley's two roommates left, and she suddenly felt abandoned. "This is crazy," she said to herself. "Because I landed a plum role in the last play I'll ever be in at Canby Hall doesn't mean my best friends have to put all their activities on hold to help me celebrate. Besides, I'm not absolutely sure I want to be in the theater forever. Maybe I'd be better off going to Iowa, and settling down like my mom. But New York is pretty fascinating, and the bright lights and the glamour . . . that is, if I'm famous."

"You're all alone." Such an affected voice could only belong to Pamela. "Don't tell me you've been deserted by your beloved roommates, and right after you heard the news about getting a part in the play. Not that it's exactly a stellar role, but it suits you." The door to 407 hadn't been closed, so Pamela felt free to invade Shelley's privacy.

"For your information, I do not feel deserted," Shelley lied, but she would never give Pamela the satisfaction of admitting it. Besides, she would defend her roommates' loyalty to the death.

"Just wondering, that's all. I guess you don't feel like talking."

"As a matter of fact, I was just about to write a letter. Do you mind closing the door?"

"If you wish," Pamela said. Then in one slow, langorous motion, she turned around and pulled the door shut behind her.

Shelley tried unsuccessfully to hold back her tears. Pamela had probably been listening to her conversation with Dana and Faith, and nothing would have given her greater pleasure than to think they weren't getting along. Shelley wouldn't go so far as to think anything was seriously the matter, but Pamela had hit a nerve. The truth was, Shelley did feel terribly alone all of a sudden.

Writing a letter to Paul isn't a bad idea, she thought, and pulled a box of stationery out of her desk. He's my safety valve, and I can get a lot of things off my chest without anyone else knowing.

Honeybear,
This has been a really crazy day. There's
good news and bad news. The good news
is I got a really good part in the school
play. The bad news is Dana and Faith
had to run off and I have no one to celebrate with. Faith is borderline hysterical
about getting her portfolio ready for
Rochester, and for the first time in ages
Dana got really annoyed with her. Now
I'm annoyed with both of them. . . . We
are all a little edgy — maybe it has something to do with last-semester blues. . . .

Shelley read over what she had written, and
decided she couldn't send such a letter. It
spelled out exactly what she was feeling, but
it was too painful to see it written down. Besides, even if it was true, she didn't want to
face it.

Just at that moment, there was a knock on
her door, and Casey charged in.

"Hey, Shel, I hear you got the juiciest part
in the play. How about coming to Pizza Pete's
and celebrating? Treat's on me!"

"Who told you?" Shelley asked brightly.
"Or are you a mind reader?"

"Two little birdies," Casey answered myste-
riously.

"Do they happen to be named Dana and
Faith?"

"You're the mind reader," Casey confessed.

"Now get ready, and I'll pick you up in five minutes."

"Thanks," Shelley murmured, not knowing whether she wanted to laugh or cry.

The one thing she did know was that her roommates would never fail her. Thinking that, she bunched up her letter to Paul and tossed it in the basket.

By the time they had trudged to Greenleaf and arrived at Pizza Pete's, Shelley's good humor had been almost completely restored. Casey marched directly to the back of the restaurant and Shelley followed, vaguely wondering why Casey was walking so determinedly. Then she saw that Tom and Keith were already in a booth waiting for them. Casey slid into the seat next to Keith.

"Surprise!" the three of them shouted in unison.

Shelley held her head with the palm of her hand, as though she might faint, but her wide grin showed how pleased she was. Then she sat down next to Tom.

"You're something else, Casey," Shelley said.

"Didn't think it'd be much of a party with just the two of us," Casey explained, "so I rounded up Tom and Keith. They were both grinding away at their books."

"If I flunk a math quiz tomorrow, it's all your fault," Tom said, grinning at Shelley. "But I'd much rather be looking at you than figuring out logarithms."

Keith said, "And I was in the middle of a paper on long-range weather patterns that would help anticipate the amount of rainfall and encourage us to find alternative ways to supply water before a shortage becomes critical."

Casey hung on every word, but Shelley couldn't help saying, "I hope I haven't interrupted some breakthrough that will benefit humanity."

"Oh no," Keith assured her seriously, "I'll finish the paper later. Nothing will be lost."

For the next couple of hours, they ate themselves silly, generally found everything they said amusing, and even had some serious discussions. Shelley was having such a good time that it was hard to believe she'd felt so rejected just a short time ago.

Tom and Shelley talked intensely about the theater, and Keith was overjoyed with Casey's response to his scientific pontificating. She couldn't take her eyes off him as he told her about "an alien tree called *Melaleuca quinquenervia*, also known as punk tree, which sucks up three times as much water as other swamp trees and therefore dries out the land."

"Fascinating," Casey purred, and snuggled closer to him.

They could easily have spent several more hours at Pizza Pete's, but curfew was at ten o'clock on week nights. Ms. Allardyce's warning to seniors about setting an example and not breaking rules was fresh in their minds.

Casey took care of the bill, and then they all buttoned up in parkas in preparation for the mile-trek back to the campus. Tom insisted on escorting Shelley to her door, even though it meant retracing his steps back to the village of Greenleaf. They tactfully let Casey and Keith get a head start. Even though kissing was forbidden on campus, there was no rule about kissing *off* campus, and that gave them a whole mile in which not to break a rule!

"This was so much fun, Tom," Shelley said. Tom had his arm around her shoulders as they ploughed their way back to Baker.

"Any excuse not to do my homework," Tom joked, and Shelley poked him in the ribs. "Only kidding, Shel. It was really a celebration for both of us. I was hoping we'd be in one more play before you graduated."

"Don't remind me," Shelley sighed. "Now everything is for the last time."

"You mean you're really not anxious to get out of here? Personally, I can't wait to graduate from Greenleaf High and just study acting. I'm going to the New Haven School of Drama, you know."

"You're lucky, Tom. Your future is all mapped out."

"Isn't yours?" Tom looked surprised. "I thought you were going home, to Pine Bluff, and all that implies."

Tom knew about Paul, and Shelley's relationship with him. Although she and Tom had been romantically involved, Tom was aware of how much Paul meant to her.

"I might go to New York and try to break into the theater." Shelley held her breath, waiting for Tom's reaction.

"More easily said than done, without any special training," Tom said honestly.

"You're a barrel of encouragement," Shelley groaned. "Anyhow, I might not do that either. I might go to the University of Iowa."

"Whatever, Shel, I'm really glad I got to know you these past couple years."

They had arrived at the front stoop of Baker, and there was no sign of Casey and Keith, who had probably gone inside.

"You sound as though we'll never see each other again, Tom."

"Don't put it like that. I'll see you tomorrow, at rehearsal." He laughed, a little nervously, Shelley thought.

"Of course," Shelley said. She sensed that Tom had been trying to tell her something, but they'd had such fun all evening she didn't want to spoil it.

"Back to the logarithms," Tom said, and squeezed her shoulder affectionately. "Sweet dreams, Shel."

"Same to you, Tom." Shelley blew him a kiss and went inside. She still felt a glow, but was more mixed up than ever about life — and Tom. Anyhow, she thought as she climbed the stairs, what started out as a bummer — with her roommates skipping off, and Pamela needling her — had turned into a great evening.

Shelley couldn't wait to tell Dana and Faith all about it, but the minute she walked into the room, something stopped her. Faith was sitting at her desk, supporting her chin with her hand, and staring into space. And Dana was brushing her hair with such fury that Shelley knew she had to be mad at something.

"Hi," Shelley said mildly. "Did I miss something?" she hoped her roommates weren't having a fight again. Twice in one day would have broken all records.

"Not what you're thinking, Shel," Dana told her. "It's that Terry O'Shaughnessy. I could kill him."

"I thought you thought he was so cute, even after you discovered he had a girl back home."

"He *is* cute, and we're really good friends, but we can't agree on anything. . . ."

"Like what?" Shelley asked.

"He thinks we should choose some punk music, or something Madonna would sing, and write words to it for Arch Day, and I think we should take a song from a Broadway musical like 'Getting to Know You,' from *The King and I*. To put it mildly, we've come to an impasse."

"Maybe you can find something in between that'll be a compromise."

"Maybe. We're meeting again tomorrow."

"That's good. At least there are two of you — not like me who all by my lonesome has to learn my lines. What you're going through is not the end of the world."

"No, the end of the world is what I'm going through," Faith sighed. "Another disaster."

"You mean you didn't like your last roll of film?" Shelley asked.

"You guessed it. I'm giving it one more try."

"It'll be fine, Faith, I know it."

Faith looked at Shelley skeptically, didn't say anything, and started to get ready for bed.

"Well, in case you're interested, I had a great time tonight — thanks to you." Shelley had to tell them about her evening. "Casey, as you know, invited me to Pizza Pete's, and arranged for Tom and Keith to be there. It was really a surprise, and the timing was perfect because I was feeling kind of sorry for myself and Pamela had just honored me with her presence, for the simple purpose of. . . ."

Shelley was inclined to babble, and she suddenly realized that neither of her roommates was paying much attention. Faith had crawled into bed and was staring up at the ceiling, and Dana was in the closet, hanging up her kilt, and not even pretending to listen.

"Anyhow, it was fun . . ." Shelley finished, and decided to get ready for bed, too. As she started undressing, she added as an afterthought, "My mom says things always look better in the morning."

But neither Dana nor Faith responded to that, either, and Shelley knew for sure she might as well be talking to the wall.

CHAPTER FOUR

"You're really stubborn, Terry," Dana grumbled.

"No, you are, Dana," Terry countered. "You just won't see my point of view."

"And you won't see mine."

Dana and Terry were continuing their previous night's discussion in the senior lounge, and each one was as inflexible as ever. They were sitting opposite each other on the floor, the coffee table between them. They had already consumed two Tabs and were nowhere near an agreement.

"Why not have something really mod, something that has meaning for our generation?" Terry asked.

"Because I personally think these punk tunes have a very short life span," Dana replied.

"So what? It's where it's at — state of the art."

"They also aren't so easy to put words to."

"That's a challenge I'm ready to meet." Terry was adamant.

"That's fine, Terry, but we can't spend every waking hour from now until Arch Day working on this song. I should be doing research for my paper on Susan B. Anthony right this minute."

"For your information, my time could be better spent, too. I haven't begun my calculus homework, which is due first thing tomorrow morning and will take me all night."

"Perhaps you would like my opinion." A silvery voice interrupted their argument.

Dana and Terry looked up, startled to see Pamela Young hovering over them. They thought they were alone, since it was three o'clock and most students were either in class or on the playing fields at that hour.

"Thanks, but no thanks," Terry growled.

"We can handle this," Dana told her.

Dana and Terry exchanged a conspiratorial smile. It was the first time they had agreed on anything in almost twenty-four hours, and they both saw the humor in the situation.

"Actually, I don't know why you're making such a big deal of all this. Who cares?" Pamela asked in her superior manner.

"We do!" Dana and Terry roared with such fervor that Pamela stiffened and blinked her eyes rapidly — a definite sign that she was unprepared for such an outburst.

"Personally," Pamela said slowly, trying to recover her composure, "I think you're over-doing it."

"We don't!" Terry and Dana spoke again in a chorus, as though they had been rehearsed.

"It's all kid stuff, anyways." Pamela was obviously annoyed and made a rapid exit. She couldn't deal with their united front.

Dana and Terry collapsed in laughter, and when they finally pulled themselves together, Terry said, "I just had a brainstorm."

Dana looked at him in amazement. "Me, too."

"You tell me yours first, Dana."

"Okay. I think maybe we *should* get an outside opinion."

"That's exactly what I was thinking," Terry shouted gleefully. "Who do you have in mind?"

"Somebody neutral . . . somebody who cares . . . somebody. . . ."

"Somebody like Alison!"

"Alison is perfect! Let's go there right now." Terry stood up and extended his hand to Dana, who gracefully hopped to her feet.

"You know," Terry said with a twinkle, "you're not as difficult as I thought."

"*Moi?*" Dana raised her eyebrows as though she was astonished that anyone could find her difficult. Then she added grinning, "Neither are you."

"Do you realize that for the last five minutes we've agreed on everything?"

"That Pamela, in spite of herself, is a force for good. They could use her at the United Nations. Everyone would be against her, and she'd unite the world!" Dana chuckled at the idea.

"That's right. She's done us a great service. Now if we can just find Alison. . . ."

"Let's go see if she's in her room. If not we'll leave a note on her door and tell her we must speak to her immediately."

"Right. This is a kind of creative emergency."

Terry took Dana's hand, and the two ran up the stairs side by side. When they got to the third floor, they both stopped dead in their tracks. "What is that?" Terry asked in a stage whisper. "Follow it and see what it eats."

"It" was Pamela Young, who was just returning from the bathroom, her face covered with mud. She must have thought that no one was around and she could apply a mud mask to her face without being seen.

Pamela was known to have tons of makeup — enough to open a cosmetic shop — and she experimented with all kinds of skin preparations. This was probably a new beauty treatment, which she never would have risked applying if she thought anyone was on the floor and might see her. It was impossible to tell if she was embarrassed because so little of her face was revealed. Her eyes, however, flashed angrily.

Dana tugged at Terry's arm, trying to get him to move. She knew it was bad enough to be seen by another girl looking so ridiculous, but it must have killed Pamela to be caught by Terry. Dana, like everyone else, couldn't stand Pamela's affectations, but at that moment she did feel a little sorry for her.

Terry, however, ignored Dana's tugging at his arm, and kept staring at this strange apparition. " 'She walks in beauty, like the night,' " he murmured, quoting Byron.

Pamela tried to speak, but her lips were caked with mud and all she could do was gurgle. In desperation she stormed into her room and slammed the door. Then Terry and Dana exploded with laughter, and the two were giggling and breathless when they arrived on the top floor. Alison must have heard them coming, because she was standing at the threshold of her door, waiting.

"Thank goodness you're here," Dana said. "We've got a problem."

"You have a rather unique way of showing it," Alison observed, smiling. "Come on in and tell me about it. I just made a new recipe for oatmeal cookies, and you can sample them."

Dana sat down on the rocking chair, and Terry made himself comfortable on the sofa that was covered with madras pillows. A couple of minutes later, Alison returned from the kitchen, passed the cookies around, and then sank into the easy chair.

"Now tell me what's troubling you."

"It's the song we're doing for Arch Day. We are at opposite ends of the pole," Dana explained.

"That's because Dana has the old-fashioned idea that a Broadway tune will be more suitable than — " Terry started to explain.

" — than some crazy punk number," Dana finished.

"I can't believe you're so establishment," Terry criticized.

"Nothing to do with that. It's just that there's a melody to some of the old tunes."

"Depends on your definition of melody."

The two of them were back to square one, but Alison got a clear picture of what was happening. "Hold it, hold it," Alison said. "I think you both have a point, but the answer is to compromise."

"Sure, but how?" Dana asked.

"Easier said than done," Terry mumbled.

"Well," Alison said, munching on a cookie, "choose something entirely different . . . something that has survived the test of time. . . ."

"We can't put words to Beethoven's Ninth," Terry joked.

"Even I wouldn't go for that," Dana conceded.

"No, but there are tried and true songs that have been popular with everyone since the late nineteenth century." Alison looked at Dana and Terry expectantly.

"Is this a form of Trivial Pursuit?" Terry asked.

"You might call it that," Alison answered.

"Give us another hint," Dana said.

"Together these two men, who were British, wrote fourteen comic operas." Then she added pointedly, "Would you call these cookies Yum Yum?"

"Gilbert and Sullivan!" Dana and Terry exclaimed at the same second.

"You got it!" Alison said delightedly.

"That's a terrific idea, Alison," Dana said.

"I think so, too," Terry agreed. "Clever music, without being establishment."

"Establishment, without being too clever," Dana said, making them all laugh.

"The next question is what tune to use," Alison said.

"Whatever madame wishes," Terry said magnanimously, tilting his head toward Dana.

"Your choice," said Dana. "I'm really so agreeable. However, I do love 'The Major General's Song' from *The Pirates of Penzance.*"

"And so do I. Now all we have to do is write the lyrics."

"That's easy. The hard part is over. If it

hadn't been for Alison, we'd probably still be battling."

"How do you do it, Alison?" Terry asked seriously. "I mean I was ready to resign. . . ."

"You were ready . . . I was going to give it one more minute," Dana said, "but Alison saved the day. What is your secret, Alison?"

"It wasn't that hard. You see, when you came barreling up the steps, giggling so much, I knew you were on the same wavelength. And even though you were disagreeing, you still were able to laugh. The rest was easy."

CHAPTER FIVE

For the next couple of days, Faith could be seen in the most extraordinary positions, clicking away. She hung from every conceivable tree, oblivious to the possibility of breaking her neck. Still, she wasn't convinced that she was ever up high enough to get a really great landscape shot. Casey suggested that she rent a hot-air balloon, and Shelley thought a helicopter would be helpful, but Faith could barely smile at their suggestions. She was too intent on her purpose to kid about it.

Faith got up very early the morning before her deadline for sending in her pictures. She didn't want to lie in bed and worry, so she got dressed, slung her camera around her neck, and went out for a walk. The campus was deserted at that hour, the air was crystal clear, and Faith felt better just moving around.

She'd almost given up on finding any new angles, when she spotted Mr. Kreevitch, the groundskeeper, in his lumber jacket and cap, atop a ladder outside the library. He was doing some electrical wiring on an outdoor lamppost, smoking a pipe and humming to himself. Just seeing him there gave Faith a good feeling. Bernard Kreevitch was an outdoorsman who took great pride in caring for the grounds.

"Hi, Mr. Kreevitch," Faith called to him, as she strolled over to where he was working.

"Morning, young lady. You're up before breakfast. About to take some pictures?" He glanced at her camera.

"I would, if I could get up high enough," she answered.

"I'd invite you to join me up here, but there's no room," he said, chuckling.

Faith was silent for a minute, and then her face lit up. "Mr. Kreevitch," she said excitedly, "you just gave me a brilliant idea. If you would loan me your ladder and show me how to get to the roof of the Main Building, I could shoot the entire campus with my wide-angle lens and — "

"Slow down, Miss. I like to keep everybody happy, but I've never had a request like this." Mr. Kreevitch had finished wrapping a wire with electrical tape, and eased himself down the ladder.

"I've got to get a really good view of this area, and the only way is to be on a rooftop. Since there aren't any skyscrapers around, a ladder might do. Please, Mr. Kreevitch, help me."

"I don't know about this." He took off his cap, and scratched his head thoughtfully. "I think maybe we should ask the headmistress. I don't want to break any rules and get you in trouble."

"I wouldn't want to get you in trouble, either, but I know we won't be breaking any rules. No one has thought to make a rule about climbing ladders or standing on roofs."

Mr. Kreevitch nodded his head and clamped his cap back on. "One thing's for sure . . . I wouldn't want you going up there by yourself. You'll be a lot safer if I go with you."

"You'll do it, then?" Faith looked so relieved and happy that Mr. Kreevitch had to smile.

"Come on, then," he said. "Let's get going before we have an audience. We can go in the rear door, up the back stairs, and right onto the roof. What some people don't know, won't hurt them."

Minutes later, Mr. Kreevitch led the way up the stairs. When they arrived at the top, he unfolded the ladder, allowed Faith to position it in different places on the roof while he steadied it, and she balanced herself on the top step. After taking a whole roll of film, Faith's fingers were numb, but she wasn't the least bit concerned. She finally had the vista she wanted captured on film, and her immediate problem was solved. Developing the roll would be easy.

Faith climbed down the ladder and vigorously shook Mr. Kreevitch's hand. "You saved my life, Mr. K.," she said.

"I wasn't about to let you break a leg," he said.

"That's not what I mean. If I didn't get any decent landscapes to send with my portfolio I might not get even close to getting a scholarship. Now, at least, I'm in the running."

"Glad I could be of service." Mr. Kreevitch looked a little bewildered, but he was used to kids not making too much sense. He folded the ladder and headed back to the stairs, with Faith behind him.

"I wish I could repay you," Faith said, when they reached the ground floor.

"Send me a picture, will you? I'd love a bird's-eye view of Canby Hall. Been taking care of this place half my life, and I've never had a decent photograph of it."

"Nothing I'd like better, Mr. K."

Faith skipped off, feeling as though she had been relieved of a great burden. When she got back to her dorm, her roommates were just coming alive.

"Where you been, Faith?" Shelley had one eye open and her voice was muffled in her pillow.

"You wouldn't believe it, but Mr. K. took me to the roof of the Main Building and allowed me to use his ladder. I took shots of the whole campus and beyond. I know I got some good stuff."

"Lucky you. Now if I could only learn my lines, everything would be coming up roses for all of us," Shelley muttered.

"You're assuming Terry and I can write a song that makes sense for Arch Day." Dana had rolled off her mattress and was doing her sit-ups on the floor.

"At least we're on an upswing." Faith, for the first time since vacation, was feeling optimistic. "You got the part in the play, Shel, and that was crucial; and Dana, you and Terry did agree on a tune, and that was crucial; and I got the pictures I wanted, and that was crucial."

"All this is true," said Shelley, "but if I don't get these bones out of bed and into some rags and over to French class . . . you know what you can do with all that crucial stuff. . . ."

"So move yourself," Faith said, and playfully tossed a pillow at her. "I'm going to skip breakfast and go to the darkroom right now. Then I'm going to call Johnny and tell him to meet me at the post office in the village where I'll mail my photographs. He made me promise I'd call him when I finished with all this. I think I was getting to be a bore. . . ."

"No comment," Shelley said, smiling, and threw the pillow back at her.

"I hear what you're saying," Faith said,

laughing. Then she grabbed her books and hurried out.

Faith, who was inclined to be a perfectionist, had to admit the photos she'd taken that morning weren't bad. She selected the best ones and created a montage that she mounted on cardboard so that one could grasp at a glance the physical essence of Canby Hall. That included everything from the dorms, buildings, barns, and stables, to the meadows, orchards, and ponds. She made a copy of the prints for Mr. K. and then raced to class.

As soon as the students were dismissed that afternoon, she signed out on the chart that hung on the bulletin board outside Alison's door. Then she went to her room and with painstaking care wrapped the prints in a special corrugated envelope that she had purchased weeks before.

"I've done the best I can," she murmured as she sealed the package. "Now I just have to wait."

Faith was lighthearted as she walked briskly into town, her "fate," as she thought of it, securely tucked under her arm. First she went to the post office, where she had the photos insured, certified, and sent First Class Special Delivery. Although Faith was conservative about spending money, no expense was too great to protect her future!

Johnny, who was working at his father's service station for a year before going to police school, was already at the Tutti Frutti waiting for her. He was in the back room, past the fountain, at what he and Faith kiddingly called "our" table. Faith smiled widely when she saw him and the two strawberry sodas he'd ordered — her favorite flavor. Johnny leaped to his feet and firmly planted a kiss on her cheek.

"Congratulations," he said.

"Not yet," she protested. "Keep your fingers crossed."

"When will you hear?"

"If I'm lucky, in about a week. Then again, it might take longer."

"Don't worry. You're really good, and you know it."

"It's not that — it's the scholarship I'm worried about. Anyhow, I don't want to talk about it, okay?"

"Okay. Let's talk about me. I just got the catalogue from my college, and I have to select certain courses. A lot of the stuff is required — like Legal Rights of Criminals, and Ballistics, and Court Procedures, but I also get to choose some courses. There's one on art and architecture that sounds interesting. Probably teaches us all the possible places criminals might hide their loot — like in the apse of a church." Johnny laughed at the idea, but Faith looked somber.

"I know you're going to be a policeman,

like my father, but I still don't like to think about it. My father died being a hero and I can't ever forget that."

"There are risks in every job, Faith. If you travel to a desk job on a New York subway in the summer and the air-conditioning conks out, you can be asphyxiated. You can work in a grocery store and be zapped on the head by a can of beans falling from a shelf. I even heard of a salesperson who was crushed at an end-of-the-season closeout sale. Did you know there are more accidents at home, especially in the bathroom, than any other place?"

"Stop!" Faith pleaded, smiling again. "I get your point. But still, I'd just as soon not talk about it."

"Let's see," Johnny said, "we can't talk about your future, because it's not definite, and we can't talk about mine, because it is. . . . I got it, let's talk about us!"

"Good idea. Do you remember the first day we met? It was right here. I was standing in line waiting to pay for my ice-cream cone, and you bumped into me with yours."

"Luckiest accident I ever had, Faith. You're my first real girl friend, you know."

"I know. I wish it could go on, and on, and on. . . ."

"Why can't it? Just because we'll be in different places doesn't mean — " Johnny abruptly stopped talking and frowned. For the first time, he was struck by the fact that they would be separated, by time and distance. Maybe only temporarily, or maybe for a year or two, or maybe forever. . . .

"What's wrong, Johnny?" This time it was Faith who was concerned about his sudden change of mood.

"Nothing . . . I mean everything. I don't want to talk about it."

"It's only fair that you tell me what you're thinking."

"You're right, Faith. It's just that. . . ." Johnny took a long sip of his soda, as though that might give him strength.

"It's just that what?" Faith encouraged him to go on.

"That I've been so busy helping out at the station, and planning for next year, and doing some preliminary reading on police procedures that I didn't take time to face the fact that you won't be around to hold my hand."

"I don't like to think about that, either, but it's a fact of life that won't go away," Faith said sadly. "If I don't go to Rochester, I'll be in D.C. next year and you'll be in New York. We might as well be on different planets if we're not in the same city."

"There's always Ma Bell," Johnny said with false gaiety.

"And we'll still get vacations. . . ."

"But it's not the same. I guess I'm some kind of idiot not to have gotten used to the idea."

"It's what's known in psychology as blocking." Faith was trying to keep things light.

"I've been in a fool's paradise, pretending this can go on forever. Even if I don't see you all the time, I know you're only a mile away. And now ... after June. ..."

"Listen, Johnny, you were the one who said you didn't want to talk about it. I'm beginning to think you were right."

Johnny nodded his head. "Let's concentrate on the time we have left together, instead of what it'll be like when we're separated."

"I think it was Eleanor Roosevelt who said, 'It is better to light a candle than to curse the darkness.' "

"That's beautiful, Faith, and so are you." Johnny reached for her hand and gently squeezed it. "Remember, Faith, no matter what happens to either of us, I love you."

"I love you, too, Johnny, and nothing is going to change that!"

CHAPTER SIX

The play had been in rehearsal ten days and everyone, except Diana Washburn, had memorized their lines. Diana was a pretty, red-haired junior who had transferred from a school in Vermont. She had the role of Alice, the lovely young girl who was engaged to Tony Kirby. Tony — played by Tom — was the son of the boss for whom Alice worked, a handsome Ivy League type, who was an idealist in spite of his stuffy parents.

Although Diana had all the talent necessary to make a good actress — poise, grace, projection — she was totally undisciplined. She believed that if she got the gist of her lines across, precision didn't matter. Shelley, who played the part of Alice's mother, was completely thrown when Diana whimsically said whatever popped into her head. Finally Mrs. MacPherson, the dramatic coach who was called Ms. Mac, and who was generally very patient, became exasperated with her.

"Diana," she pleaded after Diana had improvised wildly for the third time in one scene, "I know you're accustomed to free-form interpretation, but the playwright has written the lines a certain way and I'd rather you didn't change them. *Please* stick to the text."

"I'll try," Diana replied sweetly. "I really will. You see, at my other school. . . ."

"Never mind that. You're at Canby Hall now."

"Oh, I know, and I love it here," she said so beguilingly that everyone, except Shelley, smiled at her.

"Okay, Di, I'm glad to hear that. Now try to nail down the part and we'll run through this scene tomorrow." Then Ms. Mac turned to the others and said, "That's it for today, gang. See you tomorrow, same time, same place."

The actors got up from wherever they were sitting, and started to disperse. A few of them hung around in clusters, talking about the play and gossiping. Shelley couldn't wait to get Tom alone and tell him how happy she was that Ms. Mac had finally told Diana off.

A few days before, Shelley had complained to Tom about Diana's improvisations, and how tough it was to do a scene with her. Tom didn't seem too sympathetic, and he made some remark about an experienced actor being able to wing it, even if the cue wasn't perfect. Now that the coach had spoken out, Shelley felt she'd been justified in her complaint.

Shelley looked for Tom, and saw that he was one of several who had formed a ring around Diana. They all were laughing at something she had said. Shelley thought how she would have been devastated if Ms. Mac had chewed her out in front of everyone, and she was amazed that Diana wasn't bothered in the least. If anything, she was enjoying the attention.

Shelley edged her way toward the group, and heard Diana saying to Tom, "You're so good in the part, Tom. A case of perfect casting."

"Just because I'm handsome, witty, strong . . ." Tom said with a straight face.

There was another ripple of laughter, and Shelley could feel her face getting red. Any intention of getting Tom on her side against Diana was a lost cause. She decided to do a disappearing act before she did something stupid like break into tears.

As she hurried across the campus to Baker, she wondered why she was so upset. In her heart of hearts, she knew that Tom and she would drift apart. It was painful, though, to think that he could be attracted so soon to someone else . . . someone delicate-looking, and graceful, and charismatic — and skinny! By the time she arrived at her dorm, she had worked herself into a real state. What was so great about being cast as Alice's mother, "a round little woman in her early fifties," if that was what she was beginning to feel like?

Although it was a cool day, Shelley was steaming when she opened the door to 407. She gave off vibes that neither Dana nor Faith could miss.

"What's wrong, Shel? You look like Mt. Vesuvius about to erupt," Dana said as she looked up from her typewriter.

Shelley stormed to her corner of the room, slammed her books on her mattress, and shrugged off her parka.

"Diane Washburn looks like a fragile doll and has the sensitivity of a rhinoceros."

"What happened, Shelley?" Faith was lying on her mattress, poring over a history book that she'd propped up on her knees.

"Diana doesn't know her lines and therefore messes up mine, and even though Ms. Mac told her off, everyone else seems to think it's cute."

"Everyone?" Dana asked suspiciously.

"Tom, if you must know. I mean he must really like her. He actually defended her when I told him what I thought a couple of days ago. And today they were laughing together as though she hadn't done something terrible. Wouldn't you think that he'd be a little more professional?"

"Maybe you're overreacting," Dana suggested.

"I am not," Shelley said testily.

"Okay, okay," Dana said. "It was just a thought."

"What I think is that he's got a real crush on her, and he thinks everything she does is adorable . . . even if she ruins the play," Shelley growled.

"I don't think that's the case," Faith said. "Last Saturday night I saw Tom when I went to the movies with Johnny. He was with a girl I'd never seen before. Probably someone who goes to the same school in Greenleaf."

"Oh," Shelley mumbled. "I guess he's branching out."

"I don't know," Faith said quickly. She'd been trying to make Shelley feel better, but it had backfired. "At least he's not concentrating on just one girl."

"Terrific," Shelley groaned.

"C'mon, girl," Faith said, "it's not like me and Johnny. Even though you liked Tom, there was always Paul in the back of your mind."

"You're so sure of yourself, Faith. Just because you have Johnny," Shelley barked.

Faith slammed her book shut, sat up, and glared at Shelley. "The only thing I'm sure of is that Johnny's my only real boyfriend, and it's a lot tougher for us to be separated than it is for you and Tom. Frankly, I think Tom's doing you a favor by letting you down easy."

"When I want to know what you think, I'll ask you." Shelley bounced up from her bed and energetically started straightening the things on her desk. It was a good way to let off steam, and also to hide her sniffling. If her back was to her roommates they couldn't see the tears that were on the verge of pouring down her face.

"For the first time in my life, I think maybe I'm lucky I don't have a boyfriend." Dana was trying to be funny, and hoped to lessen the hostility that charged the atmosphere. She looked at her two friends, and waited for a response, but she was met with icy silence.

"Hey, you two," she went on, "how about listening to the song Terry and I are working on for Arch Day? It's from the Major General's song and we think it's sensational. Actually we were planning to do some final polishing, and present it to the seniors at our next meeting. But desperate times call for desperate measures."

To avoid further rejection, Dana grabbed the paper she'd been copying and plunged right in with the song. She had a lovely clear

voice and she sang brightly, even though
Shelley was still intent on her housecleaning,
and Faith had her face stuck in her book.

The senior class of Canby Hall are
models of propriety
About to take position in the
mainstream of society

The things we've learned at Canby Hall
are often indescribable
No place that we have spent these years
could be quite so desirable

With reverence and piety
And infinite variety
The senior class of Canby Hall
are models of propriety

"How's that for starters?" Dana asked.

"Very nice," Shelley answered politely.

"Good," Faith murmured in a flat voice.

"I wouldn't want you to kill yourselves
with enthusiasm," Dana quipped.

Again, silence, but Dana's tolerance for her
roommates' lack of grace had run out.

"Remind me," she said, "if I ever need a
pat on the back to make friends with a
gorilla!"

With that, she grabbed a quarter from her
handbag and stormed out of the room. She
planned to call Randy, who she could always

count on for moral support. He was a rancher, and wasn't interested in furthering his education, but Dana considered him a really good friend. She would call and ask him to go for a run with her. The weather outside would be a lot easier to take than the frosty climate in 407!

CHAPTER SEVEN

Randy was like an old shoe, solid and comfortable. After Dana and he jogged silently along the wooded paths of the campus and back to Baker House, she had cooled off.

Dana invited Randy into the senior lounge for coffee, with the idea of telling him how indifferent her roommates had been to the song she'd been struggling over. Randy would listen, and be sympathetic, she was sure. They shed their parkas, and Dana filled two styrofoam cups with coffee while Randy settled down on the sofa. She was about to say, "Shelley and Faith didn't like my song," when she realized how childish that sounded. Besides, it wasn't even true. It would be silly, and a kind of betrayal, to say anything against her two best friends simply because they hadn't praised her sufficiently about her creative effort. Instead, she asked Randy about his ranch. For the next twenty minutes, he told her in detail the plans he and his father had to expand the main barn, increase the number of horses, and build additional stables.

"We already have the architectural plans and the material ordered. There's a new kind of barn siding that is termite proof and — "

Randy stopped suddenly, aware that he'd been talking an unusual amount. He looked at Dana questioningly. "Are you really interested in all this?"

"Yes, I am," she said, thinking it was refreshing to hear about termite-proof barn siding for a change.

"I'd like to believe that," Randy said, smiling, and stood up. "Anyhow, I've got to get home now, but thanks for listening."

Randy put on his parka and Dana walked him to the front door. "Thank you for coming over. You did me a real favor."

"Always love to see you, Dana, even though — "

"Let's not get into that, Randy. We already decided that it would never work out."

"I know all that." He opened the door, turned around slowly, and said, "I hope you're over whatever was bothering you."

"What made you think something was bothering me?" Dana was amazed that Randy was so perceptive.

"Horse sense," he said, laughing, and blew her a kiss before he loped off.

Dana returned to the lounge, cleared away the cups, grabbed her parka, and climbed the stairs. Randy was a good friend, she mused, and much more than a jock who was crazy about horses. She'd been a little shocked when he first told her he had no intention of going to college, but everything seemed to fall into place for him. That was more than she could say about her own life!

Dana slowed down as she reached 407. She hoped her roommates had stopped bickering, and she opened the door apprehensively. She heaved a sigh of relief when she saw Faith was wrapping Shelley in a swath of green cloth from a bolt that Casey was holding. Shelley had decided she was going to make her robe for Arch Day. The three of them were laughing so much that for a few seconds they didn't notice Dana.

"You look like the Jolly Green Giant," Dana said, smiling at the spectacle as she walked into the room.

"How can you say that?" Casey asked, trying to look serious.

"Yes, how can you?" Faith said. Then she dropped the cloth, raised her hands, and gave a downbeat.

At her signal, she and Shelley broke into song: "The senior class of Canby Hall are models of propriety. . . ."

That made them laugh even harder, and

Dana beamed. "You've been practicing my song!"

"We didn't think you'd mind. You left it on your desk and we couldn't resist singing it for Casey," Faith explained.

Faith walked over to her desk, put some prints in a folder, and said to Dana and Casey, "I'll meet you in the dining room. I told Mr. K. I'd deliver the pictures I took of the campus. He said he'd be in the kitchen all afternoon, and I want to catch him."

"And I'd better get to the library," Shelley said.

They hurried off together. As soon as they disappeared, Dana asked Casey what miracle she'd performed on her roommates. "When I left they weren't speaking to each other."

"They weren't when I arrived. In fact, I thought something terrible must have happened."

"What did you do, Case?"

"Not much. The truth was, I wasn't in such a great mood myself. I'd come in because I felt like talking."

"You told them what was bothering you, right?"

"Exactly. We had a trouble-fest, and my problems seemed so much worse. . . ." Casey's eyes misted, and Dana was shocked. Casey *never* cried.

"You want to talk about it?" Dana asked.

"It's no secret," Casey said, swallowing hard, "and I might as well get used to the idea. Talking does help."

"Go ahead, then," Dana said gently.

"I just got a call from my mother. She and my father are going on a European buying trip in a month or so. You know, they travel all over the world buying art for their collection. Anyhow, there's some big auction going on the first week in June, in London, so. . . ."

"So they won't be here for graduation," Dana murmured, and felt a lump in her throat.

"You got it," Casey said crisply, trying to hide her hurt. "Anyhow, Faith and Shelley didn't think their problems were so enormous after hearing about mine."

"They sure aren't."

"In fact, Shelley confided that she was annoyed with Tom taking out other girls, but she couldn't really blame him since she had Paul. And then she apologized to Faith, who she admitted had much more reason to be upset about being separated from Johnny. Then the two of them felt so awful about me that I found myself in the peculiar position of trying to cheer them up. That's when we started kidding around with the material Shelley had bought for her Arch Day robe."

"You know something, Casey, I don't know what we'd do without you," Dana said.

"I don't, either," Casey agreed, trying hard

to keep up her spirits. "Would you say every cloud has a silver lining?"

"Not if I could help it," Dana said, and they both managed to smile.

Mr. Kreevitch was just packing up his tools when Faith arrived. Generally the kitchen was off bounds to students, but Faith stood at the open door and tried to catch Mrs. Merriweather's eye. Mrs. Merriweather, the head cook, was a sweet, round woman who loved the students. Everyone agreed that she would be perfect for the job if only she'd learn how to cook. She was bustling around the kitchen, peering into pots, muttering to helpers, and she finally noticed Faith. Faith held up the folder she was carrying and pointed to Mr. Kreevitch.

"Come in, dear," Mrs. Merriweather said absentmindedly as she poured too much salt into a bubbling cauldron with one hand, and waved to Faith with the other.

"You didn't forget!" Mr. Kreevitch broke into a smile when he saw Faith approaching. "Been working on this darn dishwasher all afternoon and it still doesn't work proper. Have to order a new part, I'm afraid. Anyhow, let's see what you got. There's a clean counter over here."

Faith followed him into a pantry off the main kitchen and spread the pictures on the counter top. Mr. Kreevitch gingerly picked up each print, held it in his large work hands as though he were handling a precious gem, and carefully examined it. Faith watched and waited for him to say something. He was silent for so long that she finally asked, "Are they okay?"

"Okay," he repeated so softly that she could hardly hear him. Then he dabbed at his eyes with the back of his rough hand, and with painstaking care put the photos back in the envelope. "They are beautiful."

"Thanks, Mr. K. Thanks a lot," Faith said happily. "Now I better get out of here. I think Mrs. Merriweather forgot that I'm not supposed to be in the kitchen."

"I don't think she'd mind," Mr. Kreevitch assured her. "Whenever I'm here, she offers me all kinds of treats, and I take them mainly to keep her happy. She can never do enough for me, and I know she'd be pleased that you brought me — " he scratched his head as though that would help him find the right words, and then his face lit up " — that you brought me the best present I've ever had."

CHAPTER EIGHT

For the next couple of weeks the girls in 407 were back on track. After several more rehearsals, Shelley reported that Diana had finally learned her lines, and the play was shaping up nicely.

Tom actually asked her to go with him to the Tutti Frutti after the last rehearsal. She couldn't resist the invitation, although she knew she was no longer his special girl friend. It was a wise decision, because he lavishly praised her ability to play the role of a middle-aged woman, thus bolstering her ego so that Diana didn't seem so threatening.

Dana was also feeling cheerful. She and Terry had finished the Arch Day song and presented it at the meeting of the seniors. It was unanimously praised, and even Pamela refrained from making any critical remarks. Dana and Terry passed out photocopies and

urged everyone to memorize it by the next
meeting.

Faith was busy with her photography assignments for the *Clarion* and the yearbook,
but they were a lark after the pressure she'd
felt about getting her portfolio ready for
college.

Then, to top off the sense of cameraderie,
the girls received an invitation requesting
their presence at a party to be given by the
boys of Baker. This was a first — Terry, Sheff,
and Keith had never thrown a party before —
and if the invitation was any indication, it
was going to be a blast. On a pineapple-shaped
hand-painted card, was a poem:

Shed the end-of-winter blahs
and come to our luau
Don your Polynesian garb
and prepare to do the hula

When: the last day of March
Time: nine until . . .
Place: The Place — otherwise known as
       the Senior Lounge
Dates: optional
RSVP not necessary, because who could
resist the party of the year?

The boys were absolutely right. Everyone
was in the mood to do exactly what the invitation suggested — shed the blahs. Dana,

Faith, and Shelley speculated about the party from the moment they were invited.

"Dates optional," Faith pointed out, "but it wouldn't be a party for me without Johnny."

"I wouldn't go that far about Tom, but I think I'll invite him for old time's sake," Shelley said.

"And I'll ask Randy. He's such a good friend — and, besides, I'm not interested in anyone else," Dana said.

Dana, Faith, and Shelley had received their invitations before class, and cornered Terry, Sheff, and Keith at lunchtime in the cafeteria. The girls went over to the table where they were seated and immediately volunteered to help with the food, music, and decorations. They were somewhat taken aback when their offer was refused.

"Thanks, anyways," Sheff said. "We can handle it."

"We want you to be our guest," Terry offered, a little more tactfully.

"I don't know why they can't help," Keith remarked, making his roommates sigh and the girls giggle.

"Just get into an Hawaiian mood. We'll do the rest!" Sheff told them.

"Whatever you say," Shelley said.

When they got back to their own table, Faith said, "How are we ever going to find hula skirts this time of year? Even if I could afford one, it wouldn't be in the stores now."

"I could ask my mother . . . maybe she'd know where," Dana said.

"That's crazy," Shelley exclaimed. "All we need is some straw and I'll do the rest. I'll make us identical hula skirts, and we can wear the tops of our bikinis."

"Terrific idea," Dana said.

"Where'll we get the hay?" Faith, as always, was practical.

They looked at one another hopelessly. "Hay . . . straw . . . if only there was time, I could get my brother who works on a farm every summer to send me some," Shelley mumbled.

"Wait a minute!" Dana exclaimed. "You just gave me a brilliant idea. Randy will get it for us. I'm sure he can spare enough hay for three hula skirts."

"Not necessarily . . . not with my hips," Shelley joked. "Anyhow, it'll be a good excuse for me to go on a crash diet."

"We can make some paper flowers to wear in our hair," Faith suggested. "I can see it now — something like orchids or white gardenias or red camellias."

"And we can work up a hula dance. Anything goes, as long as we wiggle and wave our arms. My father sent me a tape of Polynesian music, but I never thought I'd be using it for this!" Dana said.

"You know something," Shelley said, "I'm

really glad the boys refused our offer to help. We'll be so busy preparing to be the perfect guests, there won't be time for anything else!"

Shelley had been kidding, but the next ten days the girls were in a frenzy getting ready for the party. Dana arranged for Randy to deliver the straw and Shelley immediately began working with it. Meanwhile, Faith created exotic paper blossoms for their hair — red for Shelley, orchid for Dana, and white for herself.

Shelley ingeniously attached the straw to one of her cotton dirndls, and the effect was amazing. It looked like the real thing. When it was finished, Dana put on Hawaiian music, and Shelley donned the skirt. Then she sashayed around the room, her hips swaying and her arms imitating waves, until the three of them were roaring with laughter. Finally Shelley fell to the floor in a heap, faking exhaustion.

"That's fabulous, Shelley. The skirt's a sensation," Dana said.

"And so is your hula," Faith said. "You dance like a Polynesian native."

"You sure I don't look like a moving haystack?" Shelley asked so seriously that they all cracked up again.

Dana extended her hand to Shelley and pulled her to her feet. "You've got to teach us how to make these hula skirts. If we're going to look like triplets, we better get started."

"Dig up a cotton skirt and I'll show you how it's done. You have to doublestitch at the waist and intertwine the straw so that it's long enough. Once you get started, it's easy."

For the next few days, Dana and Faith worked furiously on their skirts. When that job was completed Dana, who was a natural dancer, taught her roommates a few simple hula steps, which they kept repeating until they synchronized. Once they had their dance perfected, Shelley said that if all else failed they could always join a chorus line.

The day of the party, the senior lounge had a sign posted: No Trespassing — by order of the management. That meant the boys wanted their decorating to be a surprise, which piqued everyone's curiosity. Even Casey, known as Girl Spy and Secret Agent, wasn't in on it.

That night, the excitement was at fever pitch. Shelley enlisted Dana's aid in choosing the right makeup.

"For once, Shel, you can wear purple eye shadow," Dana said.

"How about false eyelashes?"

"Let's not overdo it."

"We're probably going to freeze at the party," Faith said as she fastened her bikini top.

"It's worth it, Faith. Pneumonia is a small sacrifice to make for art," Shelley told her.

"I guess you're right," Faith conceded. "Anyhow, this party is going to be an original. If it's as much fun as the preparations, it's got to be a success."

"Wonder what made them think of Hawaii as a theme," Shelley mused, pinning a red blossom to her hair.

"Maybe they did it for me," Dana said "Sort of a dry run. . . ."

"It might help you make a decision," Shelley said.

"Something tells me the real Hawaii won't be anything like what we're going to see tonight," Dana said, laughing.

"We've got fifteen minutes, and I'd like you guys to check me out." Shelley stood up and slowly turned around for their inspection.

"I'd give you a ten," Faith rated her.

"Not quite. Something's wrong." Dana was frowning.

Shelley's face fell, and Dana quickly reassured her. "Everything's fine but the feet. You can't wear a hula skirt and sneakers."

"You mean I have to go barefoot?"

"If you want to look authentic."

"What about the danger of athlete's feet — or splinters — or. . . ."

"Anything for art," Faith reminded her, smiling.

"You win," Shelley groaned, and sat down to remove her shoes and socks.

"And since we want this to be world class, here's some Dragon Lady red lacquer to polish your toenails."

"Hey, me, too." Faith said. "That's one thing I didn't think about."

"You know, Dana, we really need you for the details," Shelley remarked.

"We wouldn't have a decent costume at all if it weren't for you, Shel. And those flowers you made for our hair, Faith, were inspired."

"I guess we're really an unbeatable team," Faith surmised.

"That's for sure." Dana agreed.

"Problem is," Shelley sighed, "how will I get along without you?"

They were all quiet for a minute, feeling closer than ever.

"We don't have time for sentiment," Dana said.

"That's right," Faith concurred. "And Shel, if you don't finish with that paint job, we'll be late."

"You're right." Shelley handed her the bottle of nail polish. "I almost forgot — we're going to a party!"

CHAPTER NINE

Dana, Faith, and Shelley made a final inspection of one another and at precisely eight fifty-eight headed for the senior lounge. Their dates were waiting in the hall, and applauded wildly when the "Hawaiians" came padding down the stairs. The girls were equally admiring when they saw the boys' attempt to go native. Tom, who loved getting into a role, wore a jungle-print shirt and shorts; Randy's idea of Polynesian garb was a camouflage jumpsuit; and Johnny wore cut-off jeans and a brightly-colored shirt patterned with tropical fruit. The six of them were laughing and talking nonstop as they approached the lounge, and that set the tone for the whole evening.

The second they walked in, they all knew their expectations about the party had been fulfilled. Standing at the door was a gorilla who placed a lei over each person's head as he or she entered. The heat had been turned on full blast, simulating a tropical climate, and an artificial palm tree bedecked with papier-mache coconuts was in the center of the floor.

Sheff was playing a ukelele, assisted by a tape of Hawaiian music in the background. Terry, wearing a flowered bathing suit, tended the bar that was set up at the far side of the room. He ladled out drinks from an enormous bowl of pink punch filled with spices, and served each cup with a tiny umbrella.

The guests wore mou-mous, pareas, sarongs, and caftans, but the 407 roommates were the most smashing of all in their grass skirts. Ordinarily, one would expect a housemother to be a drawback at a party, but Alison had the opposite effect. She added to the festivities by her enthusiasm, and looked like an Hawaiian beauty in a yellow halter dress, her auburn hair gilded with a garland of fresh flowers.

Michael Frank, Canby Hall's ruggedly handsome guidance counselor, was the other chaperon — as well as Alison's escort — and he supervised the refreshment table, which offered an exotic selection of dishes. He took enormous pride in describing the delectables, and it was obvious he'd had a hand in helping prepare them.

"Have some poi," he said to whoever approached, pointing to a bowl of something that vaguely resembled mashed vegetables.

Dana, Faith, and Shelley had picked up their drinks and gravitated to the table at the same time Pamela did. They hadn't noticed her entrance, but now it was hard not to stare. Pamela's idea of Hawaiian was a slinky black one-shouldered dress and red satin spiked shoes.

"Don't you look cute," she appraised the three girls condescendingly.

"So do you — for a flapper party," Shelley countered. "Maybe you're in the wrong — "

"How about some poi?" Michael interrupted. His training as a counselor warned him that there might be an explosion if he didn't intervene.

"I've never seen poi that looked like that," Pamela said. "When I was in Hawaii, I had the real thing — taro root, cooked, pounded, and kneaded to quite a different consistency than whatever this is."

"You found me out," Michael said, laughing. "This is really baked beans with brown sugar and ketchup, but it tastes a lot better than any taro root I ever had. Try it, why don't you?"

"Wouldn't think of it. This stuff is for the peasants."

"You're wrong — it's the peasants who eat taro root. . . ."

Pamela wasn't sure if Michael was kidding

her or not, but she didn't hang around long enough to find out. As gracefully as possible she slithered off and pretended not to hear the girls' barely muffled laughter.

"These pineapple boats are the real thing." Michael held up a platter of hors d'oeuvres, which the girls sampled and assured him were excellent. Then they tried the chicken wings, barbecued in Hawaiian sauce, and were helping themselves to a second portion when a creature wearing an orange beach robe, sunglasses, and a wig of long straight black hair charged up to them. They stopped eating, and tried to figure out who it was when she spoke: "Where is he? I can't find him anywhere."

"It's Casey!" Shelley squealed. "It's Casey!"

"I never would have known you." Dana shook her head in disbelief.

"What a fantastic disguise," Faith said.

"Thanks," Casey muttered, "but I think maybe it's too good. I haven't seen Keith all night, and he probably can't recognize me."

"He must be here," Dana said, "but come to think of it, I haven't seen him, either."

Casey looked imploringly at Shelley and Faith, but they both shook their heads. Then she turned to Michael, and was about to question him, when the gorilla galumped over to where they were standing.

"Have you seen Casey?" It was a rather wimpy tone for such an impressive-looking animal, but Casey thought it sounded familiar. She whipped around and squinted at the simian head.

"Keith?" she whispered hesitantly.

"Casey?" the gorilla murmured.

Casey yanked off her wig and her glasses just as the gorilla removed his head.

"Oh Keith, I didn't know for sure if it was you," Casey exclaimed and threw her arms around the hairy form.

"I should hope not!" Keith replied.

"Don't be insulted," Casey said, standing back and looking him up and down. "You're the cutest monkey I ever saw."

"I guess that's a compliment," Keith said, more bemused than usual.

"It is, it is," Casey assured him, and grasped one of his huge paws.

A group had gathered around and were riveted by the reunion, but the absurdly romantic couple were oblivious to their surroundings. They continued talking as if they were alone, and eventually walked off together while everyone who had been watching burst out laughing. But Casey and Keith couldn't have cared less. They were too involved with each other to notice that they had been the center of attention.

The highlight of the party came when Terry, acting as master of ceremonies, conducted a hula dance contest. He used a hand microphone and asked everyone to clear the center of the floor.

"We don't have an applause meter," he explained, "but Keith has an instrument that measures sound. Whoever receives the highest decibel count wins. All the brave souls among us who are willing to perform, raise their hands."

There were plenty of volunteers and, with great fanfare, Terry called on each one of them. They all got a rousing reception, but the girls in 407 — who happened to be the last — brought down the house. They kept repeating the steps they had practiced, but were so encouraged by the response that they started to improvise. Each girl took an individual turn, faking it all the way, and then the three of them instinctively went back to the original routine until the music stopped.

"No question about it," Terry announced after consulting Keith's sound meter, "the girls of 407 are the winners! Let's hear it for Dana, Faith, and Shelley!"

The crowd cheered wildly, and Terry signaled the girls toward him.

"You might think this was a set-up and that we knew who the winner would be when you see the prizes," he said. "But it's just a coincidence that the prizes are almost exact replicas of the winners, and we have three because we thought there might be a three-way tie. Anyhow, it gives me great pleasure to present these honest-to-goodness Hawaiian dolls to the girls of 407!"

He handed a small doll, dressed in a grass skirt and bandanna top, to each of the girls. Again, there was thunderous applause, pounding of feet, and ear-shattering whoops.

Dana, Faith, and Shelley glowed with all the attention, and graciously bowed to the audience. While their heads were lowered for the fifth bow, Faith whispered, "I told you we were an unbeatable team."

"You were so right," Dana agreed.

"And now the whole world knows," Shelley said proudly.

The party broke up at two o'clock in the morning — house rules — and the girls reluctantly said good-night to their dates, profusely thanked their hosts, and trudged upstairs to their room.

"Best party I've ever been to," Faith said, as she slid out of her skirt.

"I'll go along with that," Dana said, unpinning the flower in her hair.

"I'll never forget it, and I'm going to keep this prize forever." Shelley put the little Hawaiian doll on her dresser and patted the top of its head. "Means more to me than the blue ribbon I won in the 4-H sewing contest when I was in junior high."

"That's because you discovered hidden talents tonight," Dana remarked.

"Yeah, Shel, you never knew you could hula like a native."

"That's not why." Shelley turned around slowly and her eyes were glistening. "It's because — because of us."

Shelley hadn't been too specific, and an outsider would never have known what she meant, but her roommates understood perfectly.

CHAPTER
TEN

The next day, Sunday, the girls slept until almost lunchtime. As soon as they were all awake, they relived each moment of the party, discussing in depth everyone's costume; Pamela's unerring ability to say the wrong thing; how adorable Casey and Keith were together; the unsuccessful attempt of Alison and Michael to keep their romance private.

"The party came at the perfect time," Shelley remarked, still flat on her back and not making any moves to get out of bed. Dana and Faith had already gotten up, washed and brushed, and sat at their desks sipping Tabs and eating pretzels.

"Yes, it sure did. But it was a little like the last meal before facing the guillotine," Faith said.

"What are you talking about?" Shelley leaned on one elbow and stared at her roommate as though she hadn't heard right.

"This happens to be the fifteenth day of March, and that means I should be hearing about my acceptance — or rejection — from college any day now."

"Why do you have to ruin our good mood by bringing in reality?" Shelley asked, trying to make a small joke.

"Because I'm worried, that's why." Faith couldn't see anything funny about Shelley's question.

"We all had a great time last night, Faith," Dana said. "Right?"

"I'm not denying that, but that was last night and today's today."

"Listen, Faith," Shelley said lazily, "what I think I'll do is get you some worry beads. I think they're supposed to help in some mysterious way."

"You know, Shelley, you can't make a joke out of everything," Faith complained.

"I'm not trying to. I'm just . . . oh, I give up. . . ."

"Come on, Faith," Dana said. "It's normal to feel a letdown after a party — especially one as terrific as last night's."

"So all I'm doing is acting normal," Faith snapped at Dana.

"For your information, I've got plenty to worry about, too, but I don't like being reminded about my troubles." Dana frowned at Faith.

"Put your head in the sand. That's not a

bad idea." Shelley buried her head in her pillow, trying for laughs again, but this time Dana was offended.

"I'm not putting my head in the sand," she protested. "I'm just not talking about what's bothering me."

"Well, I haven't mentioned my problems lately, either — too busy making hula skirts." Shelley rolled over and faced the wall, indicating she'd had enough of this discussion.

"I think I'll go get some coffee. I need something," Dana grumbled as she scrounged in the closet for something to wear.

"I'm going to the library. There, at least, talking is not allowed," Faith said stonily.

Dana and Faith dressed in silence while Shelley pretended to be asleep. What had begun as a super warm gab fest had deteriorated into a cold quiet. It was hard to believe that in less than twelve hours, the "three peas in a pod" — as Shelley sometimes referred to herself and her roommates — could feel so distant.

For the next couple of days the girls treated one another with cordial politeness, and kept a tight lid on their emotions. As far as really communicating, they might just as well have been inhabiting separate planets. Then, a few days later, Faith received The Letter.

It was hand-delivered by Alison, who knew how anxious Faith was to learn the results of her application. Usually the mail wasn't sorted until late morning, but Alison was in the mailroom buying stamps after breakfast when she happened to see the letterhead. She hurried back to Baker, handed the letter to Faith, and then tactfully disappeared.

The girls were getting ready for class, and if Alison hadn't made such a hasty departure, she might have noticed how unusually quiet things were in 407. As it was, the girls were barely talking, but when Alison left, Shelley momentarily let down her guard and said, "It's a thick envelope. That means you're accepted!"

"Maybe," Faith murmured, trying to be cool. But her hands were trembling as she slit open the envelope.

Her roommates studied her face, trying to glean a reaction, but Faith remained inscrutable as she read the letter for the third time.

Dana couldn't bear the suspense, and finally asked, "Good news or bad?"

"Both," Faith sighed. "I've been accepted but I can only get a partial scholarship. That means I probably can't go."

"Maybe you could work this summer — make enough money to pay the difference," Shelley said.

"No way. It's just too much."

"Your mother wants you to go, doesn't she?" Dana asked.

"Yes, but she can't afford to send me."

"There must be something —" Shelley started to say.

"You don't understand. My mother is the sole support of our family. My sister is still in graduate school, and my little brother is going to boarding school. They're on scholarships, too, but it still costs plenty for clothes and books and everything." Faith was getting more and more upset.

"Your mother might think of something," Shelley persisted.

"I can't expect her to make sacrifices just so I can go to college," Faith said resignedly.

"Why don't you ask her?" Dana suggested.

"Look, it's my problem and I'll handle it. You two couldn't possibly understand what it's like to be really strapped for money. You, Dana, have enough clothes to open a boutique, and your mom is constantly sending more. And you, Shelley — well, money doesn't ever seem to be a problem for you, either."

Both Dana and Shelley clammed up. They knew that Faith was thinking she was the only one of the three who didn't have a father. She missed him terribly, and this was a painful reminder of how difficult life was for her family — and especially her mother — since his death.

"I'll call my mom now, catch her before she goes to work," Faith mumbled to herself, and stuffed her books in a tote bag. "I guess there are worse things than working during the day and going to school at night." Then she hurried out.

Dana had concentrated on brushing her hair, and Shelley straightened her bed — which was already made — while Faith was talking. She could really be stubborn and there wasn't much more they could say. Dana was still smarting from the crack Faith had made about her having so many clothes. And Shelley was hurt that her humorous remarks were taken the wrong way by both her roommates. Everyone was mad at everyone else.

Shelley gathered her belongings and put on her jacket. As if by mutual agreement, she left for class ahead of Dana. There was no point in leaving together because they had nothing to say to each other. The estrangement between the three girls was a fact of life, and as their personal problems intensified, the rift widened.

Faith's mother immediately accepted the collect call from her daughter. Her first question, even before she said hello, was, "Faith, are you all right?"

"I'm fine, mother. I'm just calling to tell you I've been accepted at Rochester, but — "

Before Faith could finish her sentence, her mother shouted, "Faith, honey, that's fantastic. Congratulations! What a way to start my day!"

"There's a problem, though."

"What's that?"

"I can only get a partial scholarship. Two-thirds of the tuition and no room and board."

Without a moment's hesitation, her mother said, "We'll find a way, Faith. Don't worry."

"But Mom, you don't understand. It'll cost thousands — just for one year."

"I know that, but we'll manage. Cut down some ways . . . even go into savings."

"I can't let you do that, mother. That savings is for you . . . for your old age." Faith was being serious.

"I'm a long way from that, honey," her mother chuckled.

"But I don't want you to have to cut down. . . . I know you, you'll give up your vacation or not buy a winter coat or — "

"Faith, you know how important I think education is. I'd make a lot of sacrifices to see my kids have the best one possible."

"You can't, if you don't have the money."

"You're forgetting one thing . . . I have a good job, and I'm not about to lose it." Then she added, laughing, "Unless I stay on the phone much longer."

Faith managed a weak laugh. "Thanks, Mom, but I can still go to night school, and make some money during the day, and live at home."

"Look, Faith, this is a wonderful opportunity, and I want you to take advantage of it."

"But I won't feel good about it if — "

"You are the most obstinate child, Faith, but I'm going to figure out something. Now please don't make any rash decisions." Faith's mother was obviously thinking that Faith might write the office of admissions and turn down their acceptance.

"I won't," Faith said lamely. "And thanks for everything."

"Thank *you*, honey. Just remember, you've made me so proud of you."

Faith hung up slowly, feeling more torn than ever. It would have been easier if her mother had been selfish and agreed that the financial burden would have been too great for her to bear. Then, at least, Faith wouldn't be so weighed down by an enormous feeling of guilt.

CHAPTER
ELEVEN

By the end of March, there were definite signs of spring on the campus. Soon the paths and walks would be lined with flowers, the pond would lose its grim grayness, and the trees would bud. All this, however, was lost on the occupants of 407, where the air was frostier than ever.

Their earlier troubles — Shelley's concern about getting a part in the play, Dana's worry about the Arch Day song, and Faith's anxiety about her portfolio — were minor compared to the monumental problems the girls were faced with now. And each one was afraid to talk about her own personal anguish for fear of being misunderstood. Instead, little things that they would previously have laughed off, became real sources of irritation: Faith blew up when she discovered her roommates had left the mustard on the radiator and it was inedible.

"I'll get a new jar," Dana told her. "No big deal."

"That isn't the point."

"What is the point, then?" Shelley asked.

"It was practically full, and that's just being wasteful. Not that you two would care about that."

That was a conversation stopper, because neither Dana nor Shelley wanted to get into another discussion about finances with Faith. Instead, the next day Dana bought a new jar of mustard and without a word or a note, left it on Faith's dresser. Since it wasn't clear who had actually replaced the jar, Faith didn't think it was necessary for her to say thank you.

Shortly after that incident, Shelley succeeded in provoking her roommates. Shelley sometimes practiced her lines aloud, and in the past her roommates had found her very entertaining. But this particular night, Dana and Faith told her in no uncertain terms to do her rehearsing somewhere else when they were trying to study.

"I have a French test tomorrow," Faith griped as Shelley worked on her delivery. "It would be a lot easier for me to pass if I was allowed to study without you emoting all over the place."

"I want to run through this one scene before I go to bed. Somewhere I read that things sink in better when you sleep on them."

"I thought you knew your lines," Dana said sarcastically, looking up from the math problems she was trying to solve. "You said it was Diana who was messing up."

"I do know my lines, absolutely cold, but I'm trying to crystallize my performance." Shelley sounded haughty, but her lips quivered.

"I don't know what you're talking about, but I wish you'd do our crystallizing somewhere else," Dana said, and turned back to her textbook.

Shelley mumbled something about how tough it was to be an artist in an indifferent environment, grabbed her towel, and headed for the door. Just before she left the room, she turned and said dramatically, "I'll do my rehearsing in the shower, where you can't possibly be disturbed."

Shelley didn't wait for them to say anything, and hurried down the hall. She was anxious to get into the shower and turn it on full blast so that no one could hear her or see her cry.

Blowing up over trivia was the girls' way of letting off steam. Even Dana, who could be counted on to remain level-headed in a crisis, was constantly on the verge of losing her temper. It was almost as though the roommates alternated being the center of a storm, and now it was Dana's turn.

It was a few days after Faith's mustard scene

and Shelley's rudely interrupted practice session that Dana released her pent-up anger. She had returned from a chorus rehearsal that had been a total disaster.

The regular conductor, Mr. Brewster, who kept things very lively, had suddenly been stricken with a virus. Since the spring concert was less than a month off, he decided not to cancel the rehearsal. Instead, he asked one of his best sopranos, Andrea Simmons, to take over. Andrea had a fine voice, and perfect pitch, but as Dana whispered to the girl standing next to her, "Andrea couldn't conduct her way out of a paper bag."

Andrea, unfortunately, was unaware of the effect she was having on the chorus. The students were always inclined to take advantage of a substitute teacher, but when the replacement was a fellow student, the result inevitably was mayhem. However, Andrea felt impelled to rehearse the usual two hours in spite of the incessant talking and giggling.

Dana was particularly annoyed because it was a beautiful, balmy day, perfect for jogging. After a half hour of being unable to follow Andrea's sloppy beat, Dana went through the motions of singing and fantasized about getting out of there and enjoying an extended run. A combination of tension in 407 and now this bummer of a rehearsal was almost too much. She knew running would help loosen her up.

As soon as the rehearsal was over, she raced

back to Baker and planned to run until it was time for supper. She bounded up the stairs and thought about the new green velour running suit she'd been saving for warmer weather. Wearing something special always gave Dana a lift, and that was just what she needed.

Shelley was sewing the hem of her Arch Day robe and Faith was doing sit-ups when Dana entered the room and went directly into the closet. No one acknowledged her presence until she emerged and inquired in a tight voice, "Where is it?"

"Where's what?" Shelley asked, not bothering to look up.

"My brand-new running suit. I've been saving it for the spring, and it's not here. Who took it?"

"Don't look at me," Shelley replied.

"Me, neither. We never borrow clothes without asking," Faith said.

"Then who did? Did you see anyone come in here?"

"Come to think of it, I saw Maggie flying down the stairs with something green just as I was coming in. Maybe she borrowed it." Faith continued doing her exercises, obviously unmoved by Dana's problem.

"My sister, Maggie? She never takes stuff without my permission."

"As a matter of fact, I was going to get Casey to help me pin this hem when I saw

Maggie go into our room. Didn't think too much about it." Shelley bit off a piece of thread and admired her handiwork.

"Why didn't you stop her? You could at least have asked her what she was doing here."

"I figured she was planning to see you. I didn't have the foggiest idea when you'd be back, but I figured she did."

"What about you, Faith. Couldn't you have asked her what she was doing with my running suit?"

"She's your sister, and I didn't think it was any of my business," Faith replied.

"I can't believe this. I just can't believe it!" Dana was apoplectic as she rushed out of the room and leaped down the stairs two at a time. Her roommates' maddening indifference was infuriating. She might as well have been dealing with a couple of robots for all the emotion they showed. If anything, they succeeded in making her madder than ever at Maggie, and she couldn't wait to get her hands on her.

As she made her way to Addison House, which was Maggie's dorm, Dana recalled how upset she'd been when she first learned that her sister was considering coming to Canby Hall. Dana didn't want her hanging around, possibly interfering with her life and her friends. Just when Dana was finally enjoying being on her own, the prospect of being saddled with Maggie was a downer.

At Alison's suggestion, Dana had invited

Maggie to visit her for a weekend. It was then that Maggie confided she'd seen drawbacks about coming, too. She didn't like the idea of Big Sister watching her any more than Dana wanted to be in that role. Once that was clear, the two girls managed to live entirely separate lives.

Naturally they didn't have classes together, and since their interests were totally different — Maggie's extracurricular activities were computer club and tennis, while Dana stuck to chorus and jogging — their paths rarely crossed. The most they saw of each other was traveling to and from New York on holidays. Then they had so much to talk about that a fellow-passenger watching them babbling nonstop would have suspected they were good friends who hadn't seen each other in months, rather than sisters going to the same boarding school.

Now, however, Dana was having second thoughts. Maybe Maggie never should have come to Canby Hall — not if she felt free to barge into Dana's closet and swipe her clothes. Who knew what she might do next? Dana was so steamed by the time she reached Addison, 203, that she didn't even bother to knock on the door.

"Who gave you permission?" she roared as soon as she entered.

"Dana!" Maggie exclaimed, looking up from her desk where she had been doing her homework. She was totally surprised because Dana never visited her. She'd come only once before when Maggie first moved in.

Maggie had never seen Dana look quite so angry, and she was glad that her roommates weren't there.

"Oh, the running suit . . . I was going — " Maggie began to explain, but Dana wouldn't give her a chance.

"What right have you to invade my closet and help yourself to my clothes?"

"Dana, calm down, will you? I can explain," Maggie said.

"No, you can't. Don't tell me you've decided to take up running — and if you have, who said you could take my new outfit, when I'm not there, without leaving a note or telling anybody?" Dana spluttered.

"Dana," Maggie said patiently, pointing to the bed where the running suit was neatly folded, "I planned to tell you about it on my way to dinner tonight. I knew you had several jogging suits, and I didn't realize this was a new one. Honest. All I did was bring it over to show my roommates."

"Huh? Since when do you show my clothes to your roommates?"

"Because we're going to a surprise birthday party Saturday for Amy who lives down the hall. She's a health nut, and everyone has to go as a veggie. We decided to go as three string beans, and we're trying to find three green running suits that match. In fact, my room-mates are going around the dorm right now trying to borrow ones for themselves. I haven't even tried yours on yet, and you can take it back. I was going to tell you about the party and everything and . . . and I'm sorry . . . but was that so awful?" Maggie was genuinely dis-mayed to see how distraught Dana was.

Dana took several deep breaths and sank down on Maggie's bed. To her own amaze-ment — and to Maggie's astonishment as well — she was blinking back tears. "I don't know, Maggie," she sighed huskily, "I guess I'm just upset these days. I wish my biggest worry was the best way to look like a string bean. I mean, you seem as concerned about that as you were about the divorce."

"You still can't get used to it, can you?"

"No, and frankly I don't know why it's so easy for you."

"Because they're still our parents, even though they don't live together . . . and they still love us."

"That's true, but it's not the same. I want them to be together — for us all to be to-gether, instead of splitting our time between them."

"I'd like that, too, but it's not going to happen."

"And then there's Eve. She's closer to our age than she is to our father's."

"That's not her fault," Maggie said, laughing. "I think that makes her more fun, and she really tries to be friendly."

"You probably wouldn't worry at all, the way I am, about whether you should live in Hawaii for a year. You'd know right away — yes or no — but I keep agonizing about it."

Maggie frowned thoughtfully and spoke slowly. "I know that's a tough decision, Dana, but whatever you do, it's not the end of the world."

Dana looked at Maggie with new appreciation. Her little sister was making a lot of sense.

"You know, Maggie, talking to you helps. I have to admit, I was ready to strangle you with my bare hands on the way over here."

"Because I took your running suit?"

"Yes, isn't that dumb?"

"Well, kind of. Anyhow, I don't really need it. If necessary, I'll wear my dark red leotard, and go as a beet."

"Never mind, Maggie. I really don't want to break up your act. You can return it to me after the party."

"You're sure?" Maggie asked.

"Positive. In fact, I'd feel awful now if you didn't wear it."

"Gee, thanks, Dana. To tell the truth, that's kind of what I expected in the first place."

"You know something, Maggie," Dana said, smiling a little sheepishly, "sometimes I wonder which one of us is the older sister."

CHAPTER TWELVE

The breach between Shelley, Faith, and Dana continued. No one was willing to make the first move that would bring them back together. If anything, each girl's position hardened as the days passed and not one of them reached out to the other.

Dana had returned to her room without the running suit, but neither Shelley nor Faith evinced the slightest interest in what had transpired between her and Maggie. Faith had not mentioned her telephone conversation with her mother, and her roommates had no intention of asking. And Shelley, who was generally a chatterbox, refused to talk about anything.

Since it was such a busy time of year, it took a while for anyone to notice the change in 407. Casey spent every spare minute with Keith, because she knew that after graduation they would be separated. It wasn't until the first

Friday in April that she got bad vibes from her friends.

After spending the evening with Keith, and although it was almost midnight, she went to the girls' room to tell them the arrangement he and his roommates had made for the next day. The boys wanted to have an exclusive picnic — just eight of them — and Casey was sent to convey the message.

Casey could see the lights were on in 407, so she didn't hesitate to charge right in and immediately rattle off the plans.

"We're all to bring sandwiches and meet at the pond tomorrow at noon. Perfect picnic weather is predicted, and if it's warm enough we can even go swimming. You can ask Johnny, Faith, and the rest of us — " She stopped abruptly and took in the scene.

Casey was impulsive, but she was also sensitive. She knew something had gone "tilt" in here. Each girl was doing something ordinary — Dana was painting her nails, Faith was going over a photo album, and Shelley was knitting — but the heaviness in the air was suffocating.

"What's wrong, you guys?" She looked expectantly from one to the other, but no one spoke. "Are you suffering from Canby Hall withdrawal symptoms? Do you hate picnics?"

"I have too much to do," Shelley muttered.

"What about you, Faith?"

"Johnny's working tomorrow and I don't

especially want to go on a picnic without him."

"That leaves you, Dana. What about it?" Casey was still hopeful.

"I'm not in the mood for a picnic."

"You're really a fun bunch," Casey groaned. "Now that I think about it, the four of us haven't done anything exciting since the Hawaiian party."

"Been too busy," Dana offered as a weak explanation.

"Yeah, that's it," Shelley said, and Faith nodded her head.

Even though Casey was their most special friend, the mutual loyalty that had bound them together for three years prevented them from telling her how unhappy they were with one another.

"You know what they say, all work and no play. . . ." Casey wanted to cheer them up, but she might as well have been trying to make a sick puppy smile. "If you change your mind, let me know." Casey was totally disheartened.

"Will do," Dana said without conviction.

Casey looked at the three glum faces and felt a mixture of disappointment and despair. She didn't know how to improve the situation, but she wasn't the type to keep things to herself. "I guess you don't want to tell me what's bugging you, but whatever it is, I think you should know you've succeeded in making me miserable, too."

The girls were jolted by that remark, and

they looked at her with alarm. Casey wasn't to blame for anything, and they all knew it. If they wanted to assure her that their "mood" had nothing to do with her, it was too late. Casey was miffed and flew out of their room at breakneck speed, before they could say anything. She had a very high threshold when it came to getting upset with her friends, but this time they'd gone too far. They were behaving like three lemons, she thought, and too sour to turn into lemonade!

The girls went back to what they'd been doing before Casey's visit, and made no comment on her or the picnic. It seemed the more important it was for them to talk, the less inclined they were to do so. Shelley, her head bent over her knitting, muttered something under her breath about dropping three stitches; Dana, who was lying on her mattress, examined her nails and remarked to herself that the color was too dull; and Faith slammed her photo album shut as though she were angry at it and started getting ready for bed.

Minutes later Pamela appeared at the half open door. "Can I come in?" she asked, and proceeded to do just that. "I'm not interrupting anything, I trust, unless you're having a seance."

The girls were still troubled about Casey, and they weren't ready to cope with Pamela.

"The silence here is deafening," Pamela commented as she walked toward Dana's corner. Then she imperiously looked over the books that were stacked on a shelf above Dana's desk.

"Do you want something?" Dana asked.

"I know you're a poetry freak, and I wondered if you have a collection of Emily Dickinson I could borrow. I personally can't stand poetry, but I have to do a paper on her."

"There's a copy on the left," Dana said. "She happens to be my favorite poet, so *please* return it in one piece."

"Don't worry. I have no intention of keeping it. The last thing I want to do is clutter up my room with books."

Pamela removed the book from the stack, walked toward the door, and turned around to look at the girls. "Something tells me the three musketeers have been squabbling. Is that right?"

Shelley was tempted to throw something at Pamela, and Faith resisted practicing her karate chop on her, and Dana bit her tongue in order to avoid calling her an impolite name. Instead, as if by mutual consent, they remained silent and didn't give Pamela the satisfaction of even looking at her. If Pamela was ruffled by their reaction, she didn't show it. "Isn't that too bad," she remarked, and then made her usual queenly exit.

For the next couple of days, the girls avoided their room as if it was a quagmire of quicksand, pulling them down. They would study in the library, or outdoors if the weather permitted. Anything to not be together. They even managed to eat at separate tables in the dining room. Because the school year was drawing to a close, they had legitimate reasons for not seeing so much of one another. Dana had extra chorus sessions, Shelley was required to attend more rehearsals than usual, and Faith was busier than ever working on the yearbook as well as the *Clarion*.

It wasn't until the end of April that Alison became aware of what was going on in 407. She knew that the girls were off in a zillion different directions because of all their activities, and that the only time they were sure to be together was on Sunday morning. No matter what the demands of their social and school life, she could corner them in their room then.

She stood outside their door, the third Sunday in April, at eleven A.M. and listened for signs of life. The only sound that could be heard was the shuffling of feet and the rustle of paper. Alison assumed the girls were just getting up, because otherwise there would be their usual animated conversation.

Alison rapped on the door and said, "It's me, Alison. Can I come in?"

"Okay," an indistinguishable voice muttered.

Alison opened the door and was surprised

to see that Faith was getting dressed, Shelley was making her bed, and Dana was at her desk reading over a paper she had written.

Alison closed the door, walked slowly into the room, and leaned against the table that was in the center. "I'm not going to play games with you," she said firmly. "I want to know what's going on."

No one said a word.

"This reminds me of your first days at Canby Hall, when you had what amounted to an armed truce. You're three years older, and I can't believe you haven't learned something about human relations in all that time." Alison was partly kidding, hoping to get a rise out of them, but that didn't work, either.

"Okay," she continued, "there are three of you and only one of me, and together you're a lot stronger than I am. If you choose, you can muddle through to the end of the year this way. However, I consider you my good friends, and I really would like to help. Based on what we've shared in the past, and because I care about you so much, I don't think you should keep me in the dark. If you don't want to talk about it, will you write down what's bothering you and let me see it? That's a good way of airing your problems, and also shows your trust in me. How about it?"

Alison waited patiently for a response, and finally Dana spoke. Dana hadn't forgotten how much better she'd felt after her conversation with Maggie, so she knew that talking helped.

"I'm willing to tell you what's bothering me, Alison. It'll help me get a few things off my chest."

"That's great, Dana." Alison smiled at her gratefully for breaking the ice.

"I don't mind talking out my problems with you, either, Alison," Shelley said. "You, at least, are understanding."

"You mean I'm not," Faith piped up.

"Or me?" Dana inquired.

"Yes, that's exactly what I mean," Shelley answered.

"I haven't found you a great source of comfort in my predicament," Dana said.

"Or in mine," Faith added. "Neither of you guys know what I'm going through. You're too wrapped up in yourselves."

"And you're not?" Shelley asked.

"Wooaaa," Alison said. "I think I'm beginning to see the light, but first — before there's a small explosion — how about coming to my room, one at a time, and letting off steam. Then maybe we can help one another — or at least have a peace treaty until graduation."

"Those two have already said they'd talk to you, and I'd like you to see my side, too. I know you're fair, Alison," Faith said.

"That's wonderful, Faith. Now shall we pick straws to see who comes first?"

"That's childish," Dana said. "It doesn't matter as long as we all get a chance to see you privately."

"Agreed?" Alison glanced at Shelley and Faith, who nodded their heads yes.

"Let's do it alphabetically — Hyde, Morrison, and Thompson," Alison suggested.

"Why not, Dana, Faith, and Shelley?" Dana asked.

Alison couldn't help chuckling. "It was you, Dana, who said the order didn't matter as long as — "

"Okay, okay," Dana conceded, and added in a low voice, "From not wanting to say anything, suddenly I can't wait."

"Come with me right now, Shelley," Alison said. "I've got some honey buns and I'll put up a kettle of fresh tea."

"*Tea and Sympathy* — that's one of my favorite plays," Shelley quipped, following Alison to the door. "Along with honey buns — that's just what I need!"

Alison laughed at Shelley's remark and held the door open for her. Neither Dana nor Faith reacted, but they both were reminded that Shelley hadn't been funny for days. This was the first sign that her sense of humor hadn't permanently gone underground. Although her roommates couldn't admit it, the ominous cloud hovering over 407 was just a shade lighter.

CHAPTER THIRTEEN

Shelley settled in the easy chair in Alison's cozy "penthouse" with the cuddly cat Dobie curled in her lap. She began talking as soon as Alison brought in the refreshments, and only took time out to sip the tea and munch on the honey buns. She complained about her roommates being edgy, her quandary about what to do after graduation, and her recent sense of isolation. It was against Shelley's nature to hold back her feelings, and now she spilled out everything. It was so easy to confide in Alison, who listened attentively, nodded her head in understanding, didn't pass judgment, and therefore was the perfect sounding board.

After a half hour of what amounted to a monologue, Shelley asked, "What do you think I should do, Alison? I really do trust your opinion."

"I can't give you a fast answer, about your

future or about your roommates. Let me see what Dana and Faith have to say. Then I think we should all get together. Three heads are better than one." Alison glanced at her watch. "I'm going to give them equal time, so plan to be back here in one hour."

"I don't think I want to tell them anything. They couldn't care less. . . ."

"You said you trusted me, Shel, so let me be the judge of that. I'll see you in an hour, okay?"

"If you say so, even though I don't think it'll do any good."

Shelley gently dumped Dobie on the floor, stood up, and carried her teacup into the kitchenette. Then she walked toward the door, turned around, and smiled at Alison. "Thanks for everything, Alison. Nothing's been solved but I no longer feel like a nonperson. I guess it's because you're the only one who's listened to me in weeks!"

"It's only the beginning," Alison said, as Shelley took off.

Dana had waited impatiently for Shelley and quickly brushed past her, without saying a word, as soon as she returned to their room. Like Shelley, she couldn't wait to unload her gripes about her roommates, and also discuss her conflicting feelings about taking a year off from college and going to Hawaii.

Dana flopped down on the floor pillows and

helped herself to one of the honey buns that were still on the coffee table.

"I know what you like to drink," Alison said, handing her a can of Tab that she'd just taken out of the refrigerator.

"You know me pretty well," Dana said.

"I thought I knew the three of you very well . . . until today." Alison had a gift for getting people to talk without asking direct questions.

"I know," Dana sighed. "You just can't believe that we could get into such a state after all we've been through together. What you don't understand is that Shelley and Faith don't care about me. I mean, they can't possibly know what it's like to be faced with my decision about moving to Hawaii. They don't know what it's like to be from a broken home."

For the next thirty minutes, with Alison only occasionally asking a question, or making an observation, Dana described her roommates' self-centeredness, the constant weighing of the pros and cons of living with her father and Eve, how alone she felt not having a boyfriend, especially when she didn't have any roommates she could confide in.

"Can you help me solve any of this, Alison?"

"I'm going to tell you exactly what I told Shelley when she asked me the same thing. I can't give you a fast answer, but I think we should all get together and talk."

"You mean group therapy?"

"Why don't we call it a rap session?"

"Whatever name you give it, it'll never work with those two."

"You may be right, Dana, but as a favor to me, will you give it a try?"

"I guess so, but that's only because of you."

"I knew I could count on you. Plan to be back here at one o'clock."

Dana pulled herself up and tossed her empty Tab can into the basket across the room. "Are you going to provide us with boxing gloves?" she asked as she started to leave.

"I was thinking more along the lines of peaceful negotiations," Alison said, trying to look serious. "Wouldn't want any of my girls receiving their diplomas with black eyes."

"I know what you mean. I don't think that would fit in with the board of trustees' image of the typical Canby Hall graduate."

Then they both laughed, and Dana left the room still laughing.

Alison looked across at Dobie, who had perched on top of her stereo. "There's hope, Dobie," she murmured. "There's definitely hope!"

However, Alison's optimism dimmed when she waited almost fifteen minutes for Faith to appear. Then she heard her slowly trudging up the stairs. It was obvious that Faith wasn't nearly as anxious to talk as her roommates had been, but Alison knew not to press her. She hadn't forgotten that Faith had agreed to come because as she had put it: "I'd like you to see my side, too."

Faith sat stiffly on the sofa, as stonelike as a sphinx, while Alison brought out fresh tea and some more honey buns.

"Help yourself," Alison said, and sat down opposite her.

"Not hungry," Faith muttered.

"Probably filled up on mustard and pretzels, if I know you. Anyhow, I don't blame you. Dana and Shelley would have stayed even longer if I hadn't set a time limit."

Faith remained tight-lipped, and Alison went on as though it didn't bother her. She would never break a confidence, but she was aware that Faith knew about the hard decisions her roommates were faced with. Letting Faith know that they had confided in her might encourage Faith to talk.

"You know, Shelley and Dana are really uncertain about their plans for next year."

"Yep."

"You, at least, know what you'll be doing. You're lucky that way."

"That's what you think." Faith had let her guard down, almost against her will.

Alison looked at her questioningly. She knew Faith had been accepted at Rochester — that was public information. But it occurred to her now that Faith hadn't registered too much enthusiasm when she'd congratulated her. At the time, Alison had attributed that to Faith's wanting to act cool.

"You're all set on your major, which a lot of kids aren't sure of when they graduate from high school. And you know where you're going."

Faith looked down and still didn't say anything.

"Well, don't you?" Alison asked softly, suspecting there was something seriously wrong.

There was a long pause, and finally Faith answered miserably, "I don't know . . . I don't know anything." Then her shoulders trembled and she quietly began to cry.

Alison handed her a paper napkin that was on the coffee table and waited while Faith wiped away the tears. "I didn't know there was a problem," Alison said compassionately.

"Neither do Shelley and Dana — or at least they can't identify with it."

"Are you sure?"

"How can they know what it's like to need money to go to college? I do have a partial scholarship, but it's still going to cost more than my mother can manage."

"I didn't know anything about that, Faith. I can see why you're upset."

Faith, who had been on the defensive for so long, suddenly felt safe. Alison wasn't giving her an argument or telling her there was nothing to worry about. She was listening, and understanding, and Faith visibly and mentally relaxed. Then she started talking and it was like a dam had burst. She didn't stop until there was a knock on the door.

Alison explained to Faith that she had urged Dana and Shelley to come back at one. "I thought it would be a good idea if you all got together and talked. Things might come across a lot different if there's a neutral listener — that's me — acting as a kind of mediator."

"I'm in a weakened condition," Faith said wryly, "so whatever you say goes."

"Thanks, Faith." Alison smiled at her warmly, and got up to open the door. Dana and Shelley silently entered the room and Alison bustled around, pushing chairs close together so that they wouldn't be too far apart physically. "Sit down, sit down," she said. "I have some wonderful cheeses that will stave off the hunger pangs."

Alison kept up a patter of small talk while she fixed a platter of exotic cheeses and crackers: She mentioned the gourmet shop in Boston where she had found them and was tempted to buy everything in sight and how Dobie was getting very fussy about what he ate.

Alison was suddenly finding her one-sided conversation embarrassing and she decided to keep quiet. She carried the cheese tray in, placed it on the coffee table, and sat down on the sofa next to Faith.

The silence was unbearable, and Alison was beginning to feel defeated. She looked at each girl, and her eyes finally settled on Dana, who she regarded as a natural leader. If only she'd say something, then. . . .

"You didn't get us all here to talk about cheese," Dana said.

Alison heaved a sigh of relief, and smiled gratefully at Dana, who had given her the perfect opening. "I got you all together so you could hear each other out."

"It takes two to have a conversation, unless you like talking to yourself," Shelley said. "It's not like playing air guitar."

Alison chuckled out loud at Shelley's description, and in spite of themselves, Dana and Faith almost smiled.

Shelley was encouraged to continue: "You, Dana, never did tell us what happened with Maggie and the running suit."

"Personally, I didn't think you were interested."

"Well, you know I'm the curious type. What did?" Shelley asked.

"She wanted to borrow it so she could go to a party as a string bean. I guess I overreacted, like Faith did about the mustard. Incidentally, Faith, you never bothered to thank me for replacing it."

"How did I know it was you? There wasn't a note or anything."

"It had to be me or Shelley. You had a fifty percent chance of being right on the first try."

"Okay, Dana. I guess I didn't feel like saying anything about anything."

"That's for sure," Shelley chimed in. "You didn't even tell us what your mother said about the scholarship."

"You didn't ask me."

"It was up to you to talk about it, I thought."

"You really want to know?"

"Course I do."

"Me, too," Dana said. "I was a lot more anxious to hear about that than I was about being thanked for a jar of mustard. But you were so touchy. . . ."

"My mother wants me to go — in fact, she insists. I've spoken to her several times, and she's already arranged for a loan. That, plus digging into her savings."

"That's terrific!" Dana exclaimed. "So why aren't you thrilled?"

"Because I feel guilty."

"You can pay her back," Shelley said.

"If I could pay her back, I wouldn't have the problem."

"I don't mean now, I mean later — after you graduate and get a job. I know you'll be an outstanding photographer one day and make oodles of money."

"That's a fantastic idea," Dana agreed. "You

could have a long-term IOU. Pay off the loan
and replenish the savings after you're rich and
famous. Knowing you, Faith, you'd never go
back on your word."

Faith's face lit up with a wide grin. "I never
thought of that. It would certainly end my
guilt trip." Then she added, with unchar-
acteristic shyness, "Thank you, roomies . . .
and thanks for the mustard, Dana."

"Our housemother said three heads were
better than one," Dana remarked, looking at
Alison. "I guess you were right."

"I just had a hunch," Alison said.

"I wish it would work for me." Dana
sounded wistful.

"Why wouldn't it?" Faith asked. She was
so happy to have found a solution to her own
problem, that she couldn't wait to help the
others. "Why don't you give us a chance,
Dana?"

"You already know my problem — should
I go to Hawaii or go to college in the East
next year? I'm beginning to sound like a
broken record."

"What is it you want to do most?" Shelley
asked.

"I want to do both," Dana replied without
hesitating.

"You still can, but not at the same time,"
Faith said.

"I already know that."

"Look, Dana, more than anyone I know,

you like new adventures, and you're being offered one on a silver platter. What you have to remember is that your father might not be living in Hawaii for more than another year. College will be there forever!" There was no question in Faith's mind what Dana should do.

"Hmmm, I never thought of it that way."

"Faith's right, Dana," Shelley said. "This might be the very last time in your entire life you'll be able to live in Hawaii for a year. It'll be an experience to tell your grandchildren! And you've already got a drop-dead hula skirt."

Dana was thoughtful and muttered to herself, "They're right. Might be my last chance for Hawaii." Then, in a normal voice, she asked pointblank, "What do you think, Alison?"

"I think Faith and Shelley are making a lot of sense. Living in a totally different environment is an opportunity you may never have again. And, to tell the truth, colleges are very pleased to have students postpone going for a year — especially if they plan to do something new and different."

"That does it! I'm going to Hawaii!" Dana smiled with delight. "Now that I've made the decision, I can't understand why I was so torn. It's like I've been offered the best of both possible worlds and I was too dense to see it."

"I guess Alison is definitely right about the three heads," Faith said.

"It'll take more than three to help me," Shelley said. "My problem is so complicated."

"Can't decide between living in the Big Apple and having a career on Broadway, or going to the University of Iowa. It's sort of like what I was faced with," Dana observed. "Except, of course, I'm not going to be on my own in Hawaii, which makes it a lot easier."

"That's true. And as you know, I'm not one of the world's greatest loners. Can you imagine me holed up somewhere, no friends, no family, and no job?"

"No way!" Dana and Faith exclaimed.

"I already know I can't make it in the theater without a lot more training. Tom said it first, and I really resented it. But once I got used to the idea, I realized he wasn't trying to hurt me. He was just being honest."

"Seems like your problem is solved," Faith said.

"Yes and no. You see, if I go to the University of Iowa, Paul is going to pressure me to go steady. That way, I'll lose my independence. It was okay when I was here, thousands of miles from home, for me to go out with other boys. But if we're in the same state, he'll get the idea I'm his girl exclusively."

"Not if you spell it out to him," Dana suggested.

"Tell him you don't want to go steady," Faith advised.

"What if I lose him? I love Paul, but he's

very old-fashioned. He's not going to like it if — " Shelley's bottom lip began to quiver.

"It's a risk . . ." Dana said.

"If you mean enough to each other, you don't have to worry. That's what Johnny and I say," Faith confided.

Shelley held her head, as though that would help her think. Finally she took a deep breath and made a pronouncement. "You're right. It's a risk I have to take. Living in New York would be a copout, a way of running away from making a commitment to Paul. I can see now it isn't what I want to do. I want to go back to Iowa and go to the university. There are plenty of theater courses there I can take. If Paul doesn't approve of the new me, we're not meant to be."

"That takes guts," Dana said. "But you can do it."

"You sure can," Faith confirmed.

Shelley looked appreciatively at her roommates, gulped hard, and managed to say, "I knew I missed you two lately, but I didn't realize until now how much."

"We all need one another," Dana said, "but we forgot that for a while."

"Alison didn't forget," Faith reminded them. "She made all this happen today."

"I'll take the credit," Alison remarked gleefully. "In fact, if you'd continued the way you were going, you would have made me a liar."

"How so?" Dana asked.

"We wouldn't do that," Faith said.

"Never," Shelley agreed.

"I'll explain," Alison said, her eyes twinkling mischievously. "Yesterday, Ms. Allardyce and I were going over the rooming assignments for next year. It's not easy, you know."

"What's that go to do with us making you a liar?" Shelley asked.

"Everything," Alison answered. "You see, I maintained that the girls in 407 were the ideal roommates. Even though you're each coming from a different place — and I don't mean just geographically — the differences have made you strong. Hate to sound corny, but because of them, you've enriched one another's lives. I said you were the perfect example of what we should look for in matching roommates."

"Hear that!" Faith exclaimed proudly. "We're the ideal!"

"I guess it's because we're basically so intelligent and understanding," Dana added, smiling.

"You're forgetting one thing," Shelley said, her eyes filling with tears. "It's because we love one another."

CHAPTER FOURTEEN

Dana, Faith, and Shelley were tighter than ever after their rap session with Alison. They didn't refer to the unbearable strain they'd been under, but each girl was aware of how close they'd come to losing one another. They'd learned, painfully, that their friendship not only helped them endure any personal ordeal, but was a source of joy. Room 407, once again, became the place for fun and laughter.

The first thing the girls did was let Casey know that the freeze was off. That very day, after seeing Alison, Shelley was sent as their representative to invite Casey to their room.

Casey wasn't one to hold a grudge, and she went willingly. The minute she walked in, she knew the bad vibes had evaporated. Casey didn't ask any questions, but her friends felt compelled to apologize for their rude behavior and explain themselves.

"I thought maybe I'd done something wrong," Casey said after she heard their stories.

"You didn't do anything wrong, Casey," Dana assured her.

"Not at all," Faith affirmed, "but I was afraid you thought so."

"I think that made us all feel bad," Shelley said.

"Thank goodness." Casey sighed happily, basking in her friends' affection. "There was a real gap in my life, not being able to talk to you guys. Also, I couldn't figure out why none of you wanted to go on the picnic."

"The truth is, I love picnics!" Shelley explained. "But it wouldn't have been much fun if we weren't speaking."

"I love picnics, too. I just used Johnny not being able to go as an excuse," Faith admitted.

"And I said I was too busy," Dana said. "Actually, I'm never too busy for that kind of fun."

"I guess one of the things I missed most was having you guys to talk to." Casey's eyes sparkled.

"That's the second time you've said that. I have a feeling you have something to tell us," Dana observed. "You're our informer around here, and without you we don't know anything."

"Don't tell us P. A. is getting married!" Faith said.

Casey shook her head. "Nothing like that. It's something to do with me."

"Spill it," Shelley said. "We've done nothing but talk about ourselves."

"Remember how upset I was about my parents not making it to graduation?"

"How could we forget?" Dana asked.

"Made our problems pale by comparison," Faith said.

"Well, they're still not coming, but my favorite aunt and uncle will be here. My Aunt Barbara is my mother's sister. She and her husband don't have any children of their own, and they've always doted on me. They planned to come all along and were going to keep it a surprise. But when Barbara heard my parents would be in Europe, she decided to let me know ahead of time. I found out last week and was dying to tell you."

"That's so great!" Dana shouted.

"Fantastic!" Faith said.

Shelley started to say something, but couldn't get the words out. Then she burst into tears.

Casey looked shocked. "I thought I was giving you good news, Shelley. What's the matter?"

"It's such good news that I can't help crying."

"But why?" Casey asked.

"First, because I'm so ashamed of the way

we acted. We were so selfish," Shelley sputtered between sobs. "And second, because I'm so happy you won't feel like an orphan on graduation day."

"That's exactly how I would have felt," Casey admitted. "Anyhow, that's all ancient history, and I think this calls for a celebration."

"What should we do?" Shelley asked, pulling herself together. "Pizza Pete's?"

"Something more exotic," Dana said.

"I'm for that, but my pocketbook isn't," Faith sighed.

"I have the perfect place — and the money to pay for it!" Casey looked triumphant. "My parents were so guilty that they sent me a hundred dollars to make them feel better, and told me to spend it on anything I wanted. There's nothing I'd like better than treating my friends to a pigout."

"We'll eat ourselves silly with that kind of money," Dana said.

"There's no danger of that if we go to the place I have in mind," Casey said.

"You going to fly us to Paris for a French gourmet meal?" Dana chuckled at the absurdity.

"Not quite," Casey said, "but almost as glamorous. There's a new Indian restaurant in Greenleaf, and I've heard they serve everything laced with gold. With very little effort, we can blow the whole hundred dollars."

"Wouldn't you rather buy something for yourself — something really special you can have always?" Faith asked.

"There's nothing more special to me than you three. Whatever I can buy will wear out or I'll lose it, but an evening with my closest friends is a memory I'll have forever."

There were less than six weeks left of school, and the days weren't long enough. The school year was ending, and that was acceptable, but it was impossible to believe that the roommates' life together was almost over. There was so much to do to wind up the year, not the least important studying for final exams. Faith had nightmares about not passing French; Shelley's struggle with math intensified; Dana was more anxious than ever to maintain her high average to show that postponing college didn't mean she would goof off.

The girls stayed up later than usual in order to prepare for finals and still have time to talk. It was with a combination of regret and relief that the extracurricular projects that demanded so much of their time had ended.

Dana was thrilled that the spring concert was so successful. The chorus and orchestra did excerpts from *The Messiah*, and afterward at the reception in the gym Mr. Brewster made a brief speech. He was a very tough taskmaster, and to everyone's astonishment he said he'd never had a better group of singers. Dana make a point of thanking him for a wonderful experience, and then quickly turned away before she dissolved in tears. It suddenly struck her that never again would she be singing with the Canby Hall chorus.

The following week was Shelley's big moment. The play had been rehearsed to perfection, but there was no guarantee that last-minute butterflies in the stomach, or knees that had turned to jelly wouldn't take over. Shelley suffered from both possibilities, and was so nervous before she went on that she thought she might faint. Ms. Mac tried to reassure here that the symptoms weren't unusual. She didn't believe her for a minute, but once she was on stage they magically disappeared. She got completely immersed in her part, lost all her self-consciousness, and didn't flub a single line.

When it came time for bows, Shelley received a standing ovation and when Keith presented her with a huge bouquet of wild flowers — obviously hand-picked — the applause was thunderous. Shelley was thrilled, but a little suspicious because she knew her fans — Dana, Faith, Casey, Keith, and his roommates — were responsible. However, when the review by an impartial critic appeared in the *Clarion* two days later, she no longer had reason to doubt the audience's reaction. The review described Shelley as "the find of the evening. Her role as Penelope Sycamore, the ditsy mother, was a tour de force. It was all the more spectacular because Miss Hyde had to project as a woman in her fifties."

After seeing that in print Shelley's confidence in her acting ability was strengthened, and her self-image improved as well. "Now I'm ready for anything!" she told her roommates.

Faith was the last of the three to wind up her nonacademic project. She worked on layouts and prints for the yearbook every free minute. She was flattered that the faculty advisor wanted her in on all last-minute decisions, but she was relieved when the yearbook was finally "put to bed." There were only two weeks until finals, and she needed at least that much time to cram.

The girls were tempted to talk and giggle more than ever, as if to make up for lost time, but each one was deadly serious about doing well on the finals. Therefore they set a limit on any unnecessary conversation until they'd put in several hours of real study every night. They even refused to break up the routine by going to town and splurging at the Tutti Frutti. For once, hitting the books took priority over anything resembling a good time.

The finals were scheduled for the last week in May. After that, there was still Arch Day and graduation to look forward to. But the anxiety about doing well overshadowed everything else, and for all the seniors, it was work, work, work.

When the last exam was taken, the students tore out of the classrooms and whooped with joy. Dana, Faith, and Shelley found one another on the campus where everyone was discussing how hard or how easy the questions were. The girls linked arms, all talking at once, not caring a bit that no one was listening. They were headed for Baker when Sheff, Terry, and Keith came bounding up to them.

"We're having a celebration tonight," Sheff said. "We'll start in our room and take it from there."

"Is it okay if I invite Johnny?" Faith asked.

"Of course," Keith answered, "and I'll invite Casey."

"Maybe we'll turn it into a midnight picnic — sort of make up for the one we didn't have," Terry quipped.

"Sounds great," Dana said.

"Anything sounds great today," Shelley exclaimed. "I even think I passed my math!"

"And I'm positive I didn't fail French." Faith looked radiant.

"Maybe exams are a good thing — we feel

so wonderful when they're over," Shelley remarked.

"Sort of like hitting your head with a baseball bat — it feels so good when you stop," Sheff said.

This elicited a series of groans from the girls, and they mutually decided it was time to leave.

"Later," they yelled, running off, and talking all the way to their dorm.

CHAPTER FIFTEEN

The girls decided to dress for the occasion, which meant wearing their best jeans and shirts, and putting on makeup — something they didn't take time to do during the crunch of exams. After Faith arranged for Johnny to meet them, they coralled Casey in her room and the four of them descended on the boys. Alison, in keeping with the house rules, was already there as chaperone, and everyone greeted one another like long-lost cousins. Even though Johnny and Alison didn't have the same reason to rejoice as the others, the sense of euphoria was contagious.

The boys served sodas and potato chips, and when everyone had something in their hand to drink, Terry suggested there be some toasts proposed. "I'll go first," he said, "to show you how it's done. . . . Here's to the most promising seniors of Canby Hall!"

"And their friends!" Faith said, looking lovingly at Johnny.

"And their housemother!" Casey added.

They all got into the spirit and there was an endless stream of self-congratulatory remarks: "To the greatest!" "The best!" "The brightest!" They went on and on, outdoing one another with praise.

When the supply of Tabs, potato chips, and toasts dwindled, Sheff said, "It's time to move on. Next stop, Greenleaf village!"

"Let's go," several people shouted at once.

Then the group leaped to their feet, dumped the empties in the basket, and waited for Alison who couldn't resist puffing up the pillow she'd been leaning against.

"Come on, Alison. Stop behaving like a housemother," Terry teased.

"For that remark, I'm not going with you!" Alison pretended to be insulted.

Sheff said, "You've got to come!"

"That's right," Dana said. "We want you to."

"Who's going to keep us out of trouble?" Casey asked.

"I'm flattered," Alison said, "but when you told me there was this 'emergency party' I was just starting to write my end-of-the year recommendations for improving dorm life. It's due tomorrow, and I wouldn't want it to be late. I'll probably be up half the night working on it."

"We'll bring you a banana split," Shelley said.

"Thanks anyway. It's getting close to bikini weather, and I don't need any extra pounds," Alison said, grinning.

Everyone chuckled, and Johnny said, "Faith told me you were a one-of-a-kind housemother. Now I know what she was talking about."

"I appreciate that," Alison said. "Now you better get going so I can get to work."

"Where are we going first?" Keith asked, once the group was assembled outside.

"I think we should take a walk around the campus. It's the most beautiful time of the year and we've been too busy to sniff the flowers," Dana said.

"That's a spectacular idea. Let's have a twilight nature stroll. I'll show you the way." Terry motioned everyone to follow his lead.

"Sort of a sentimental journey," Shelley sighed romantically.

For the next half hour, the eight friends ambled along. They headed first for the skating pond, passing the chapel, then circling the stables and orchards. They savored every tree and shrub along the wooded footpaths as though they were seeing them for the first time.

Dana and Shelley rhapsodized about the beauties of the Canby Hall campus; Keith offered some technical information about the flora and fauna of the New England region while Casey looked at him adoringly; Faith and Johnny held hands and made an occasional comment to show they were still on the planet Earth; the usually flamboyant Terry was relatively quiet, deep in his own thoughts. When the light began to fade, everyone was quite subdued, experiencing in their own way the bittersweet knowledge that this was one of the last times they would all be together.

Terry took them through the iron gate that led to the public road, indicating that the "tour" was over. Sheff, always cool and confident, would never allow his heart to rule his head no matter how sentimental he was feeling. He was sensitive to his friends' mood, but he wanted the evening to be fun.

"The first leg of this trip was perfect," he said, when they hit the main road. "Now let's plan to live it up in the big city of Greenleaf."

"I'm for that! The sentimental journey was getting to me." Dana expressed what everyone else was thinking.

"It's too early for dinner," Faith said.

"Even I'm not hungry, although that might change by the time we get into the village." Shelley was only half kidding.

"There's the latest Michael J. Fox movie at the Lyceum. It starts at eight and we can eat after. How's that for living it up?" Casey asked. "All in favor say 'aye!'"

There was a chorus of "ayes!" and the group traipsed into town, singing and joking, their high spirits restored. Once again they reveled in the freedom of school being over and knowing that for the next few days they could dedicate themselves to having a good time.

They bought tickets and found empty seats in the balcony where they could all sit together. The movie was a hilarious family comedy, with a combination of slapstick scenes and amusing dialogue that had the Canby Hall contingent falling out of their seats with laughter. When it was over, they were feeling more devil-may-care than ever.

"Next stop, Pizza Pete's. Before I faint." Shelley stood outside the movie house, clutching her forehead and fluttering her eyelids.

"That would be so inconvenient," Terry said, deadpan. "I guess we'll have to carry you."

He winked at Sheff, and they both surrounded her, swept her up, and started walking.

"You're too slow," Shelley yelped, struggling to get out of their arms. "I'll do better under my own steam."

"If that's how you feel . . ." Terry began. Then he and Sheff exchanged a look and at the same time seemed magnetically attracted to a clump of bushes next to the moviehouse. There they unceremoniously dumped her.

A small crowd had gathered and was fascinated by the scenerio.

"Almost as good as the movie!" one person commented.

"Better," said another.

"This is real-life drama," said a third.

Meanwhile, Casey and Keith had managed to pull Shelley into an upright position. Shelley grinned and brushed herself off.

The spectators applauded and chuckled, while Shelley and company all laughed. "Another great performance!" Dana remarked, which prompted even more applause.

"Thank you, thank you," Shelley said, turning to her admirers. "Now what can I do for an encore?"

"You can lead the way to Pizza Pete's," Sheff answered, "before one of us really does pass out."

"I hear what you're saying," Shelley said, and ran off with her friends following.

Everything struck them as funny, especially when the eight of them squeezed into a circular booth at the back of the restaurant that was meant to accommodate only six bodies. Then they had a lengthy discussion of how many and what kind of pizzas to order. The waiter, a young man with a remarkable level of tolerance, waited patiently and even offered his opinion. They finally ended up with eight small pizzas, all different, and agreed that there be a mutual exchange of slices.

"Next stop, Tutti Frutti," Shelley said, when the last bite had been polished off.

"I'm for that!" Faith said.

"Do you realize what time it is?" Dana asked. "If we flew back to the dorm right now, we'd just make it before curfew."

"Let's live dangerously," Casey piped up.

"I'm willing. We'll be a little bit late, that's all," Sheff said.

"Whatever Casey says suits me." Keith put his arm around her shoulder.

"I'm game," Terry said. "One problem, though. We can get past the guard, but how will we get into the dorm, which will be locked?"

"No problem." Casey grinned like a Cheshire cat. "Remember when I was grounded for climbing in and out of the dorm at all hours by way of the maple tree outside my window?"

"That was one of your more imaginative capers," Faith said. "But the branches of the maple tree were cut down, making it no longer climbable."

"I know, but I discovered a new escape hatch — up the fire escape and into the girls' bathroom. The window is always open in this weather, and it'll be easy."

"Hate to sound like a wet blanket, but remember what Ms. Allardyce said about setting a good example," Dana pointed out. "If we're discovered, she might do something that would make us wish we hadn't broken a rule."

"She won't find out. Let's do it!" Sheff was enthusiastic.

"It'll be exciting!" Shelley said. "Besides, we're already past our curfew."

"That's a very good argument," Dana admitted. "Might as well count me in."

"Let's get going," Casey said.

After Keith made some speedy calculations on his calculator, and each person contributed the correct share of the bill, they paraded down the street to the Tutti Frutti. It was well after midnight when they finished a variety of elaborate concoctions and left the ice-cream parlor. Then they reconnoitered on the sidewalk, and Johnny wished everyone luck, as though they were going into battle, gave Faith a quick hug, and said good-bye.

The troops bubbled with a combination of high spirits and apprehension. Talking was an outlet for their nervousness, but when they neared Canby Hall, Terry warned them to keep quiet.

"If we act like we're not guilty of anything, the guard — Mr. Grady — won't ask any questions. He's a man of few words, and all he cares about is keeping out strangers. He knows we're all students."

Terry led the way, and when they approached the iron gate, he casually said, "Good evening, Mr. Grady. Nice night, isn't it?"

"Sure is," Mr. Grady answered, and held

the gate open until they walked past him. When they were a safe distance away, they waited for further instructions from Casey, who whispered, "Follow me."

Then the gang fell in behind her, and silently marched to the fire escape that led to the girls' bathroom.

"What if the window isn't open?" Shelley breathed apprehensively.

"Then we're in deep trouble," Casey answered, keeping up her bravado. "I'll climb up first and cough three times if there's no problem getting in and the coast is clear. Give me a boost, somebody."

Sheff promptly lifted her up to the first step, and the others watched breathlessly as she negotiated the climb to the fourth floor. After an interminable wait, which was actually less than five minutes, Casey coughed three times. Then one after the other, they climbed the stairs, successfully crawled through the window, and tried desperately not to laugh hysterically at the situation — four girls and three boys standing in the girls' bathroom after hours.

"I'll check the hall," Faith volunteered. "Make sure no one is wandering around. Then the girls can wait while the boys slip downstairs."

Faith returned a few minutes later, and motioned the boys out. Terry, Sheff, and Keith gave the "thumbs up" sign and smiled broadly as they hurried past Faith.

The girls finally relaxed, and headed for 407. They kept their voices low, and congratulated one another for pulling off the caper of the year.

"This was the best one ever," Casey bragged, "because we were in it together."

"We needed your expertise," Dana said.

"What a way to celebrate!" Shelley exclaimed.

They had arrived at the door, which was slightly ajar, and Faith stopped short. "Something's funny," she whispered. "The door was closed and the lights were off when we left."

"You're right," Shelley gasped. "I think somebody's been here."

"There's only one way to find out," Dana said, and pushed open the door.

Before they had a chance to say or do anything, Pamela Young, wearing a satiny cream-colored dressing gown, floated ghostlike toward them from Dana's corner of the room.

"What are you doing here?" Shelley squeaked. "It's way past midnight."

"I know. I came around eleven-thirty to return Dana's book. I couldn't believe you were all out at that hour."

"Well, we're back now, safe and sound," Faith said, "so you might as well leave."

"In due time. You see, I was worried when

you weren't here, and I just had to tell Alison."

"You what?" Dana roared. "You told Alison?"

"Seemed like the sensible thing to do."

"How could you? You might have waited, or . . . or," Shelley sputtered with rage.

"Or what?" Pamela raised her eyebrows indignantly.

"Or not done anything to get us in trouble," Casey growled.

"How did I know that something awful hadn't happened? I felt it was my duty to. . . ."

"You might have guessed that since four of us were missing, we hadn't been kidnapped," Dana said sarcastically.

"I didn't know what to think," Pamela responded.

"Where's Alison now?" Faith asked.

"Well, after checking everyone's room, she discovered that Casey and the boys were missing, too. I suppose she's at Allardyce's now."

"Oh no," Dana sighed, and sank down on her mattress. "This is too awful."

"This is the absolutely worst trouble I've ever been in," Casey mumbled.

"We could get kicked out of school, and not be allowed to graduate," Shelley whimpered.

"That probably won't happen, but we might not be able to take part in the Arch Day ceremony," Faith said. Then she looked daggers at Pamela and added, "Thanks to you."

"That's right . . . the most exciting event of the year and we might not be there," Dana murmured.

"I'm sorry, girls, but I did what I thought was best." Pamela moved toward the door, and just as she was about to leave the room she turned around and said, "I almost forgot, Dana; thanks ever so much for the book."

CHAPTER SIXTEEN

As soon as Shelley was sure Pamela was gone, she wept openly. Dana, Faith, and Casey were too distraught themselves to offer her any comfort, but they didn't hesitate to give vent to their feelings about Pamela.

"I'd prefer to do battle with a hungry lion," Faith commented.

"She makes a nest of hornets seem appealing," Dana said.

"I wonder if Pamela eats nails for breakfast," Casey mused.

"I wouldn't be surprised. And she probably has ice water instead of blood running through — "

Before Dana could finish her sentence, Alison walked into the room. She looked grim and her voice was steely. "I can't believe it. I just can't believe it. I just saw the light in the boys' room, so I knew you had returned. Why did you do such a harebrained thing?"

"Because . . . because we're stupid," Shelley said, still sniffling.

"I had a hunch we'd live to regret it," Dana murmured.

"We just got carried away," Casey explained.

"What's going to happen to us?" Faith asked.

"I don't know," Alison answered. "It broke my heart, but I had to tell Ms. Allardyce. I've already rounded up the boys and I'm going to personally escort you to the headmistress's house."

"Is she mad?" Shelley asked.

"What do you think?" Alison replied.

The answer was so obvious that no one bothered to say anything.

"Let's get going," Alison ordered. "Terry, Keith, and Sheff are waiting in the hall."

The girls glumly followed Alison down the stairs. They exchanged uncomfortable looks and a few anxious words with the boys, and then proceeded to Ms. Allardyce's house. They resembled a funeral procession, quiet except for an occasional cough and Shelley's uncontrollable sniffling.

Alison rang the bell of the headmistress's gracious colonial home, and Ms. Allardyce promptly opened the door. The other-worldly quality of this unbelievable experience was compounded by her appearance. For the first time, she was seen by the students with her hair down. Her silvery blond hair, which was always swept back in a severe French twist, now cascaded down to her shoulders in soft waves. She was wearing a pale-blue velour caftan that enhanced her ethereal appearance. It was difficult to determine if she was angry or sad or both when she said in a low but stern voice, "Come in, please."

Ms. Allardyce led the way into her beautiful living room furnished with gleaming antique tables and chintz-covered chairs, sofas, and love seats. Then she told the assemblage to sit down, walked toward the fireplace, and leaned against the mantel while the group settled down awkwardly and waited for the onslaught.

Ms. Allardyce got right to the point: "You realize, seniors, that you have not only violated several rules — the minor infraction of forgetting to sign out being the least — but you missed curfew by more than two hours, you broke into the dorm by illegal and possibly dangerous means, and the boys were in the girls' bathroom, which until today I believed was an inviolate law. Have you anything to say?"

Terry took it upon himself to speak first. "There's no excuse, Ms. Allardyce, except that we were celebrating finals being over. We started out walking around the campus, because we wanted to enjoy it one last time together. . . ."

"And then we went to the movie," Casey said. "That was my idea, but I guess it wasn't a very good one since we got out so late."

"And then we went to Pizza Pete's," Sheff said, "and the Tutti Frutti. We wanted to do all our favorite things. . . ."

"You didn't realize how late it was?" Ms. Allardyce asked.

"We did," Dana replied without hesitation. "We knew at Pizza Pete's that we'd never make it back before curfew, but we decided to take the risk."

"It was my fault, really," Casey said. "I convinced everyone that we could climb in the bathroom window from the fire escape."

"It was all our faults," Faith insisted. "No single person should take the blame."

"That's true," Keith said. "We were like a molecular force, gathering momentum."

"What's going to happen to us?" Shelley asked.

"What do you think would be appropriate?" Ms. Allardyce answered.

"We could do community service, if we weren't graduating," Terry suggested. That was his not-too-subtle way of asking if they were, in fact, going to graduate.

Everyone held their breath while Ms. Allardyce took what seemed an excruciatingly long time to reply, "But you are graduating."

The offenders visibly relaxed, overjoyed that they had been spared the worst. However, there was still the possibility that they would be deprived of taking part in Arch Day. That was a ritual that emotionally — although it didn't affect their future — was at least as important to them as the graduation ceremony. As if to dispel any remote hope that Ms. Allardyce had forgotten about this rite, she said, "Arch Day is the day after tomorrow. I know how much that means to you." There was an implied threat in that statement, but everyone was too afraid to ask her to elaborate.

She looked intently at each student's face. "One thing I can say is that you have been completely honest about tonight. Also, I'm pleased to see how loyal you are to one another. I shouldn't be surprised, because I've been told that you are excellent dormmates. I know, too, that you have made a positive contribution to the school. However, the honor of Canby Hall must be upheld."

"We know that, and that's why we're so sorry for what we've done." Dana spoke for all of them.

"We've loved it here." Shelley had finally stopped crying.

"It's been a home to me," Casey said.

"These really are terrific kids," Alison said. It was the first time she'd spoken since they'd arrived, and her words had a powerful effect on everyone.

Ms. Allardyce said nothing, but turned around and gazed into the unlit fireplace. She was obviously weighing all the factors, and trying to decide what action to take.

The wait, again, was painful. Finally she turned around and said, "To say that I'm disappointed in you is an understatement. As for the proper punishment. . . ." She paused.

"Anything, but don't take away Arch Day!" Shelley blurted out.

Ms. Allardyce ignored Shelley and continued: "I hope you've learned never again, in your future life, to make rash decisions. Regarding an appropriate punishment . . . my guess is you've suffered enough tonight."

"You mean . . . you mean. . . ." Casey was afraid to ask the crucial question.

"I mean I am human, you know, and I'm not about to deprive you of the privilege of participating in the school's most significant ceremony."

There were whoops of joy and screeches of relief, with everyone shouting their thanks. Shelley leaped up, impulsively threw her arms around Ms. Allardyce, and kissed her on the cheek. "We'll never forget this," Shelley cried.

"There, there, dear, let's not overdo it," Ms. Allardyce said. She gently pushed her away and swiftly walked out of the room, but not before Shelley noticed that the frosty headmistress had tears in her eyes.

CHAPTER
SEVENTEEN

T he next day the only subject the girls in 407 could talk about was their escapade, the hairy moment when Ms. Allardyce was making up her mind about what sentence she would impose, how close they came to not taking part in Arch Day. They started talking about it from the moment they awakened, which was after eleven, and were still going strong an hour later when they made a few tentative moves about getting up.

"We've got to do something special for P.A.," Dana proposed, as she rolled off her mattress.

"She was terrific," Faith said, doing some knee bends. "Do you realize how we would have felt if. . . ."

"I can't bear to think about what might have been," Shelley said, stretching her arms. "And I agree with Dana, we should do something to show our appreciation."

"Send a plant or a book?" Faith suggested.

"That's always nice, but not too original," Dana said.

"You know something," Shelley said, "I saw a new side to P.A. last night. Underneath that tough exterior, she's a pussycat. I have a feeling no one's ever said anything nice to her. . . ."

"Maybe we could write her a letter — a love letter would be overdoing it, but how about a 'like' letter."

"That's not a bad idea, Faith," Dana agreed. "And we could all attach our signatures."

"I've got an even better idea!" Shelley exclaimed. "Since she didn't take Arch Day away from us, let's dedicate our song to her. I know the boys will agree, and the rest of the seniors won't care."

"Fantastic!" Faith said. "It'll probably be the first time any student has done anything but complain about P. A."

"I think that's so great . . . better than anything else we could do," Dana agreed.

"What'll we say?" Shelley asked.

"Can't make it too sweet or sentimental, because we don't want to embarrass her," Faith remarked.

"You're right about that," Dana said.

"Why don't we just say something like 'Thank you, Ms. Allardyce, for everything,' or 'We'd like to dedicate our song to the head-mistress.' "

"That's simple enough, Shelley, but I think it should have a little more subtlety," Faith commented.

"You're the poet, Dana," Shelley said, smiling, "you come up with something."

"I'm thinking . . . waiting for the Muse." Dana sat down on her chair and closed her eyes. Seconds later she leaped up and shouted,

"I've got it, I've got it! 'We are dedicating our song to Ms. Allardyce, who knows why.' "

"That's perfect!" Shelley cried.

"Exactly the right tone. Nobody will object," Faith said.

"And P.A. can read into it as much feeling and sentiment as she wants."

The girls were delighted with themselves and couldn't wait to tell Casey and the boys the idea. They were galvanized into action, got dressed, and went to the senior lounge, which was the hangout for coffee whenever there were no classes.

Sure enough, Casey and the boys were clustered together in one corner of the room. They were so intent on their conversation that the 407 girls practically had to hit them on the head to get their attention.

"We're racking our brains about doing something for P.A.," Terry explained. "Any ideas?"

"Already decided . . . if you all approve," Dana answered.

Then Shelley told them their plan, and the response was unanimous. "Brilliant!" Sheff said.

"Dana, you announce it before I give the signal to start singing," Terry suggested.

"Okay," Dana agreed. "It's the least I can do."

"And I'll arrange to have the whole program taped. That way P.A. will have a permanent record," Keith said.

"Oh Keith, you're a genius," Casey piped up, causing a ripple of laughter.

"Now that that's settled, what'll we do today?" Sheff asked. "Go swimming in the pond? I don't think there are any rules about that."

Faith winced at the idea. "Don't be funny. I'm still emotionally wiped out from last night. I think the most exciting thing I want to do is take some close-ups of the flowers."

"All I'm ready for is some serious knitting," Shelley said. "I want to finish the sweater I'm making for Paul's birthday before I get home."

Casey turned to Keith. "Today is perfect for me to give you your first guitar lesson. How about it?"

"Love it," Keith replied.

"I'm going to curl up with a good book," Dana said.

"I guess I'll try to scrounge up a snappy game of Ping-Pong or croquet. If anyone's interested —" Sheff stopped short, tilted his head toward the door, and whispered, "Look who just came in."

"The villain," Shelley said. "She must be dying of curiosity."

"Let's pretend nothing happened," Faith said. "That'll kill her, for sure."

"We'll just act normal — you know, like real people," Terry joked.

"Just keep talking," Sheff advised, "and try not to stare."

They did exactly that and it wasn't long before Pamela wandered over and greeted them. "Good morning, all."

"Hi!" Casey said brightly.

"Another beautiful day," Dana remarked. "We've certainly been lucky on the weather."

"Might even go swimming." Shelley flashed her theatrical smile at Pamela.

"It's so great to have a totally free day," Terry said.

"The only thing we have to get ready for is Arch Day tomorrow — and that's not hard to take," Faith commented.

"Arch Day," Pamela repeated. "You'll be getting ready for Arch Day?"

"Certainly. Aren't you?" Sheff registered alarm.

"Well, yes, but I just wasn't sure that you all. . . ."

"Watch it!" Shelley cried out. "You're about to spill your coffee."

Pamela's cup was precariously tilted, and spilling was a distinct possibility. She quickly pulled back her cup, and in the process splashed coffee all over her white silk blouse.

"Now look what you've made me do," she roared angrily, and rushed off.

"I think we upset her balance," Shelley surmised, trying not to giggle.

"That is a marvel of understatement," Terry said, and then they all collapsed in laughter.

"Rise and shine, rise and shine!" Shelley shouted.

"Huh?" Dana groaned, and pulled the covers over her head.

"What's all the noise about?" Faith mumbled sleepily.

"It's Arch Day, remember? And you told me you wanted to help me with the flower-picking."

"That seemed like a good idea last night when I was wide awake." Dana slowly swung her legs off the mattress.

"You must have caught me in a weak moment," Faith said, rubbing her eyes. "But I did promise. . . ."

"You'll love it once you get started. Mr. Kreevitch has already installed the wooden arch on the stage. That was the hard part."

"It doesn't begin until three o'clock, and

it's only ten." Dana squinted at the clock on her desk.

"There's still plenty to do. We have our regular crew, but we need more hands to clip flowers and branches."

Shelley tucked her T-shirt in her jeans, raked her hair with her comb, and headed for the door.

"I'll bring my Scotch tape," Faith volunteered. "You can use it for attaching."

"And Elmer's glue," Dana added.

"What it takes is rope and baling wire," Shelley said seriously.

Then she saw Dana and Faith smiling indulgently, and realized she was being kidded. "You two are too much," she laughed. "I'll be expecting you in the maple grove in twenty minutes."

There was a low buzz of excitement in the cafeteria during lunchtime. Mrs. Merriweather had extended herself to make this a special meal, because she knew the importance of the day. The result bore a vague resemblance to meat loaf, and something that looked like gray mashed potatoes, but food was very unimportant at that moment. Even Shelley was too excited to care.

As soon as lunch was over, Shelley hurried to the auditorium and with the rest of the committee decorated the arch with the leaves and flowers that had been cut that morning and kept in containers of water. Then she raced back to Baker where her roommates were in various stages of undress.

"The arch is so beautiful," she raved, flopping down on her mattress. "All purples, pinks, reds, and white, and luscious green foliage. It's like something out of a dream."

"I can't wait to see the finished product," Dana said, "but you better stop emoting and get ready."

"We've already had our showers," Faith said.

"Is that a hint?" Shelley asked, smiling, scrambled to her feet, grabbed her towel, and rushed out.

When she returned, Dana and Faith had slipped on their green robes and were making last-minute touches to their makeup. "This will be the first time in history that you're ready ahead of me," Shelley observed. "We've got a whole half hour to kill."

"That's exactly what we're doing," Faith said. "I've had my contacts in for hours and my Afro has never been better combed."

"And I'm experimenting with two shades of eye shadow. One is sea-green, and the other is emerald forest. Since I can't decide, I'm going to use both," Dana said.

Finally the three of them were ready, stood in front of the mirror, and decided there was absolutely no room for improvement.

"Time to go," Dana announced, and the others followed her out of the room. They walked rather solemnly across the campus to the main building. While the classes took their assigned seats in the auditorium, the accompanist, Miss Smith, played the Triumphal March from *Aida*. The music was stirring and created just the right tone for the occasion. Then the light were dimmed, and Ms. Allardyce, wearing a yellow linen dress, her hair once again severely coiffed, walked onto the stage.

"This is your moment," she said simply. "Let Arch Day begin."

The freshmen who were sitting in the front rows marched onto the stage. They realized both the solemnity and joyfulness of the occasion. Since they'd heard so much about Arch Day and this was their first time, they were understandably nervous. Some of them twitched restlessly until Miss Smith played the introduction to their piece.

Their choice was "Climb Every Mountain," which they sang with fervor. The audience was genuinely touched and applauded enthusiastically as the freshmen walked through the arch, signifying their advancement to the next class. Then they returned to their seats, unable to stop smiling, deliciously pleased with themselves and their new status.

The sophomores were the next ones to take their places on the stage. A small, dark-haired girl in the front row stepped forward and made an announcement. "We are going to recite 'The Road Not Taken' by Robert Frost."

In perfect unison the class began. When they finished, the audience was quiet and reflective, and then applauded loudly.

After they walked through the arch and once again sat down with the students, it was the juniors' turn. They wore bright red, a color that reflected their strong, affirmative feelings about becoming seniors. They gave an inspired rendition of "We Are the World," swaying to the music and belting out the lyrics with gusto. The audience was caught up in their jubilant mood, and had to restrain itself from singing along. The importance of graduating to the senior class was shared by every Canby Hall student.

The seniors were the last ones on the program. As soon as they were in place, Dana stepped forward, glanced at Ms. Allardyce, who was sitting on the side, and then addressed her comments to the audience. She spoke slowly, and with careful enunciation, wanting to impress the students with her brief remarks: "We would like to dedicate our song to our headmistress, Ms. Allardyce . . . who knows why."

Ms. Allardyce smiled, a Mona Lisa smile, which particularly delighted certain members of the class. There was something outrageously wonderful about sharing a secret with the imposing headmistress.

Dana stepped back in position, Terry indicated to Miss Smith that they were ready, and the class began to sing. The parody was a smash, and the listeners rose to their feet, clapping in appreciation. Then, according to tradition, the seniors crossed beneath the arch, but instead of returning to their seats in the auditorium, they passed through a door on the stage that symbolized their entering the "real" world.

A hush fell over the audience, for everyone realized that for the seniors, Canby Hall days had ended. What awaited them was awesome — new, exciting, but unknown.

CHAPTER EIGHTEEN

It was the day before graduation and Dana, Faith, and Shelley had spent the morning packing their clothes, making the painful decision of what to throw out, clearing their shelves and walls of all the things that had made the room unmistakably theirs. They had promised one another they wouldn't do anything resembling fun until all the hard work was finished. Then, when the last item was packed, they allowed themselves the luxury of a long shower.

When they returned to the room, Shelley insisted they try on their blue graduation robes.

"We tried them on yesterday," Faith reminded her. "They didn't grow in the closet overnight."

"You never know," Shelley said. "Remember, my reputation is at stake."

"If you put it like that. . . ." Dana walked

to the closet, carefully pulled out the three robes, and draped them over the chair.

"I'll try mine on first," Shelley volunteered, "and you can tell me if there's anything wrong."

She slipped the robe on, and, not bothering to put on her shoes, twirled around.

Dana appraised her and then said, "Perfect."

"You look like a barefoot dream," Faith laughed.

"Don't you think I should wear my purple plastic beads and my orange earrings to jazz it up?" Shelley asked with a straight face.

"No!" Dana and Faith shouted vociferously.

Shelley burst out laughing, and her roommates realized she had been kidding them. "If nothing else, I've learned something from you guys in three years. Anyhow, can't you find anything wrong?"

"Nothing," Dana assured her.

"How will it look when I waltz across the stage for my diploma?" Shelley sashayed across the room, pretended to accept her diploma from an imaginary school official, and made a deep curtsey.

Dana and Faith were laughing at her bizarre antics when there was a knock on their door.

"Come in," Dana called. The girls were expecting Casey, and were surprised to see an unfamiliar face.

"Hi," a tall blond girl said. "My name is Jane Barrett. I know who you are."

Jane looked around the room coolly. "I'll be moving in here next year and wanted to see what it was like."

Dana, Shelley, and Faith were momentarily speechless. How could anyone take over their room? This was their territory and they were shocked to think that anyone would invade it. The three looked at the girl with disbelief.

"You don't mind, do you?" Jane asked. "I want to try to decide how to fix it up."

Dana took a deep breath. "Well, sure," she managed to say. "Go ahead."

Jane walked around the room, looking at it possessively, unaware of the effect she had on the roommates. The impression she made wasn't improved when Jane said, "These black walls will have to go. I can't imagine living with them."

The roommates exchanged a look and shrugged.

"This room is meant for three, you know," Faith said.

"Not next year," Jane said. "I'll have it all to myself. Thanks for letting me see it. It helped me decide what I want to do with it." She headed for the door.

When Jane had gone, Shelley shook her head. "I can't believe her."

Dana grinned. "You know who Jane Barrett is, don't you? One of the rich Barretts. Boston Barretts. Her grandfather gave the school the money to build Barrett Hall."

"All *that* in *this* room. And she says she's going to be here alone," Shelley said.

"Never," Faith added firmly. "They'll never let her have this room alone."

The graduation ceremony was everything it should have been. The day was perfect, the speeches weren't too long, and the seniors glided across the stage to receive their diplomas without a single flaw. Afterward, the reception in the park around the wishing pool took on the quality of a Victorian tea party — except for all the hugging and kissing, and the congratulations that echoed across the campus.

Everyone in Faith's, Shelley's, and Dana's family were there for the occasion. Dana's father, without Eve, had flown in from Hawaii. It was wonderful and weird for Dana to see her divorced parents together, but she tried to dwell on the positive aspect — that they both loved her.

Some of the Oakley Prep boys, especially Bret Harper, who was the Canby Hall heartbreaker, came to kiss the girls — including Dana — good-bye. Dana felt a much greater wrench saying good-bye to Randy, for she considered him a real friend. Tom was there, and Shelley was pleased that when he wished her luck and kissed her on the cheek, she wasn't the least bit undone. She knew she had really gotten over him. Faith and Johnny were another story. They moved away from the crowd so they could be alone for a few moments and just hold each other. Then they kissed good-bye, whispered "I love you," and tearfully parted.

The girls of 407 were overwhelmed by their emotions when they returned to their room to change their clothes and do their last-minute packing. They tried desperately to keep up their spirits.

"Just think," Faith remarked, folding her graduation robe, "I'll never have to worry about French idioms again."

"Right, and I won't have to stay awake all night, cramming for a math test." Shelley stepped into her new seersucker skirt, which belonged to what she described as her "travelin' suit."

"And no more boring assemblies before we've even had breakfast," Dana said. "Remember how — "

Before she could finish, Shelley's brother, Jeff, shouted outside their open window, "Hurry up, Slugger, or we'll miss the plane to Des Moines."

Shelley leaned out the window and yelled back, "Hold your horses." Then she slipped on her jacket and turned to her roommates. "I've got to leave now," she said, trying to be brave.

It was just too much for all of them and the three girls burst into tears. Then Dana and

Faith surrounded Shelley, and they embraced for the last time.

Without another word, Shelley picked up her suitcase and slowly walked out of the room.

"There'll never be friends like us," Dana called after her.

"Never," Faith said in a firm voice.

Shelley nodded her head but didn't look back, while her roommates watched until she was out of sight.

JUNIOR HIGH

Coming soon from Scholastic — just in time for the back-to-school season — a brand-new series, JUNIOR HIGH!

Meet the latest crop of Cedar Groves Junior High eighth-graders on their very first day of school. Join them in the chaotic cafeteria, the crowded corridors, the craziness of new classes. Get to know the students — from inseparable best friends Nora Ryan and Jennifer Mann, to the impossible class nerd Jason Anthony; from rich-and-knowing Denise Hendrix, to sports-maniac Mitch Pauley and sarcastic Lucy Armanson. Share experiences with these eighth-graders — the triumphs and setbacks, the friendships and first loves, the adjustments, the fun, and the occasional pain. Most of all, become a part of Cedar Groves Junior High, and the nonstop action that happens there.

You won't want to miss JUNIOR HIGH!, so watch for it as school begins!

Read All About
The Girls of Canby Hall!

☐ 40078-9	#1	Roommates	$2.25 US/$2.95 Can.
☐ 40079-7	#2	Our Roommate Is Missing	$2.25 US/$2.95 Can.
☐ 40080-0	#3	You're No Friend of Mine	$2.25 US/$2.95 Can.
☐ 40081-9	#4	Keeping Secrets	$2.25 US/$2.95 Can.
☐ 40082-7	#5	Summer Blues	$2.25 US/$2.95 Can.
☐ 40083-5	#6	Best Friends Forever	$2.25 US/$2.95 Can.
☐ 40084-3	#7	Four Is a Crowd	$2.25 US/$2.95 Can.
☐ 40085-1	#8	The Big Crush	$2.25 US/$2.95 Can.
☐ 33399-2	#9	Boy Trouble	$1.95
☐ 33400-X	#10	Make Me a Star	$1.95
☐ 33401-8	#11	With Friends Like That	$1.95
☐ 33472-7	#12	Who's the New Girl?	$1.95
☐ 33685-1	#13	Here Come the Boys	$1.95
☐ 33707-6	#14	What's a Girl To Do?	$1.95
☐ 33759-9	#15	To Tell the Truth	$1.95
☐ 33706-8	#16	Three of a Kind	$1.95
☐ 40191-2	#17	Graduation Day	$2.25 US/$2.95 Can.

Scholastic Inc.
P.O. Box 7502, 2932 East McCarty Street
Jefferson City, MO 65102

Please send me the books I have checked above. I am enclosing $_____
(please add $1.00 to cover shipping and handling. Send check or money order—
no cash or C.O.D.'s please.

Name_____

Address_____

City_____State/Zip_____

CAN 862   Please allow four to six weeks for delivery.

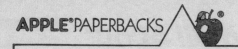

APPLE®PAPERBACKS

Mystery! Adventure! Drama! Humor! Apple® paperbacks have it all!

NEW APPLE® TITLES! $1.95 each

☐ QI 32877-8   **Tough-Luck Karen**   Johanna Hurwitz
☐ QI 33139-6   **Bummer Summer**   Ann M. Martin
☐ QI 33271-6   **The Telltale Summer of Tina C.**   Lila Perl
☐ QI 33300-3   **Encyclopedia Brown Sets the Pace**   Donald J. Sobol
☐ QI 33103-5   **Tarantulas on the Brain**   Marilyn Singer
☐ QI 33298-8   **Amy Moves In**   Marilyn Sachs
☐ QI 33299-6   **Laura's Luck**   Marilyn Sachs
☐ QI 32299-0   **Amy and Laura**   Marilyn Sachs
☐ QI 32464-0   **Circle of Gold**   Candy Dawson Boyd
☐ QI 32522-1   **Getting Rid of Marjorie**   Betty Ren Wright

BEST-SELLING APPLE® TITLES

☐ QI 32188-9   **Nothing's Fair in Fifth Grade**   Barthe DeClements
☐ QI 32548-5   **The Secret of NIMH™**   Robert C. O'Brien
☐ QI 32157-9   **The Girl with the Silver Eyes**   Willo Davis Roberts
☐ QI 32500-0   **The Cybil War**   Betsy Byars
☐ QI 32427-6   **The Pinballs**   Betsy Byars
☐ QI 32437-3   **A Taste of Blackberries**   Doris Buchanan Smith
☐ QI 31957-4   **Yours Till Niagara Falls, Abby**   Jane O'Connor
☐ QI 32556-6   **Kid Power**   Susan Beth Pfeffer

📖 **Scholastic Inc.**
P.O. Box 7502, 2932 E. McCarty Street, Jefferson City, MO 65102

Please send me the books I have checked above. I am enclosing $_____
(please add $1.00 to cover shipping and handling). Send check or money order—no cash or
C.O.D.'s please.

Name_____

Address_____

City_____State/Zip_____
APP851   Please allow four to six weeks for delivery.